J-Boys

Kazuo's World, Tokyo, 1965

For
John and Lily
with love

— Anna, Ken and Isamu

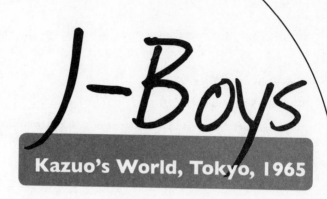

J-Boys

Kazuo's World, Tokyo, 1965

Shogo Oketani

**Translated from the Japanese
by Avery Fischer Udagawa**

Stone Bridge Press • Berkeley, California

Published by
Stone Bridge Press
P.O. Box 8208
Berkeley, CA 94707
TEL 510-524-8732 • sbp@stonebridge.com • www. stonebridge.com

J-Boys: Kazuo's World, Tokyo, 1965

Cover and text design by Linda Ronan.

First edition 2011.

Printed in the United States of America.

2015 2014 2013 2012 2011   10 9 8 7 6 5 4 3 2 1

LIBRARY OF CONGRESS CATALOGING-IN-PUBLICATION DATA
Oketani, Shogo.
   J-Boys: Kazuo's world, Tokyo, 1965 / Shogo Oketani; translated from the Japanese by
Avery Fischer Udagawa.
      p. cm.
   Summary: In mid-1960s Tokyo, Japan, where the aftereffects of World War II are still
felt, nine-year-old Kazuo lives an ordinary life, watching American television shows,
listening to British rock music, and dreaming of one day seeing the world.
   ISBN 978-1-933330-92-1.
   [1. Family life—Japan—Fiction. 2. Friendship—Fiction. 3. Schools—Fiction. 4. Tokyo
(Japan)—History—20th century—Fiction. 5. Japan—History—1945-1989—Fiction.] I.
Udagawa, Avery Fischer, 1979– II. Title. III. Title: Kazuo's world, Tokyo, 1965.
   PZ7.O4148Jad 2011
   [Fic]—dc22
                              2011010543

CONTENTS

ACKNOWLEDGMENTS

The author would like to thank Leza Lowitz, Yuto Dashiell Oketani, Avery Fischer Udagawa, Ralph McCarthy, Motoyuki Shibata, Ken Rodgers, John Einarsen, Matthew Zuckerman, Trevor Carolan, Joe Zanghi, Suzanne Kamata, Tom Baker, Jasbir Sandhu, Holly Thompson, Susan Korman, Stephen Taylor, Mayumi Allen, Art Kusnetz, Deni Béchard, Donald Richie, Yelena Zarick, and especially the great team at Stone Bridge Press—Peter Goodman, Linda Ronan, Noriko Yasui, and Jeanne Platt—for their tireless efforts to bring Kazuo's world to life.

The translator would like to thank Shogo Oketani and Leza Lowitz for the opportunity to translate *J-Boys: Kazuo's World, Tokyo, 1965;* Dr. Angela Coutts and Dr. Thomas McAuley of The University of Sheffield for valuable feedback; and her husband, Kentaro, and young daughter, Emina, for their vital encouragement and support.

Grateful acknowledgment is made to the editors of the following publications, where stories from this collection previously appeared, sometimes in different form—*Wingspan, Kyoto Journal, Yomimono, Another Kind of Paradise:*

Acknowledgments

Stories from the New Asia Pacific (Cheng and Tsui)—and to Printed Matter Press.

About the photographs, sidebars, and J-Boys website

All the photographs in this book come from the collection of Shinagawa City (Shinagawa Ward) in Tokyo, where *J-Boys* is set. They were taken from the mid-1950s through the 1960s and show activities and scenes just as they looked when the stories in this book took place.

You will find many sidebars throughout the text. These contain definitions of Japanese words and information about Japanese things that you may not be familiar with. Words in **boldface** have sidebars nearby. There is a glossary at the back of the book for quick reference.

Explore the world of the J-Boys, learn more about the author, and find resources for teachers at a special website for this book, j-boysbook.com.

Two boys hopping on pogo sticks in Tokyo.

The Tofu Maker

Kazuo stood in front of Yoshino's **Tofu** Shop, an old metal bowl under his arm.

"Hey there, Kazu-chan," the owner of the shop said as soon as he had spotted him. "Running errands for your mother again today, eh? That's a good boy."

Kazuo grinned shyly at Mr. Yoshino. The older man had tied a towel into a headband around his closely cropped white hair. His eyes shone in his wrinkled face.

Yoshino's Tofu Shop was in the heart of the West Ito shopping area, in the Shinagawa Ward of southern Tokyo. It had a large tin water tank out front and a stove inside that was black from years and years of boiling soymilk.

Four or five housewives stood before the store with Kazuo. Like him, they had come to buy tofu for the evening's dinner.

As he took his customers' orders, Mr. Yoshino dipped his hand into the tank's ice-cold water. Slowly he drew out blocks of tofu, being careful not to break them. As Kazuo

Tofu
Bean curd. Tofu is made from soybean milk that is processed and pressed into soft blocks. Tofu originated in ancient China and then spread to Korea and Japan. It is very low in calories and is often used in vegetarian dishes.

waited for his turn, he watched Mr. Yoshino's hand. It always looked red and swollen, almost chilblained, from being plunged into the frigid tank day after day. Kazuo did not care much for tofu with its slightly bitter taste and strong soybean smell. He'd leave it on his plate, unless his mother was in a bad mood and threatened that he couldn't watch TV until he ate it. Then he would hold his breath and gulp it all down without chewing. The good thing about tofu was that you could swallow it without tasting it and you wouldn't choke.

Kazuo's father, who worked two train stops away at the Nihon Optics factory, couldn't get enough tofu. The soft tofu from Yoshino's store was his favorite, and it rarely failed to appear on the family dinner table. Kazuo's mother shopped

A greengrocer's stall in a Shinagawa Ward shopping district.

for the day's dinner on her way home from work, but she couldn't take the metal bowl with her. So, except on Wednesdays, when Yoshino's Tofu was

-chan A friendly and informal suffix used for younger kids or girls.

always closed, buying tofu in the afternoons was Kazuo's job. Now that he was nine, his mother told him, he was old enough to manage this sort of thing.

Kazuo thought that he could be a tofu maker someday, if it meant working only in the summertime. But he'd decided that he could never handle it in the winter. He would almost certainly give in to the cold and bring the tofu out of the water too quickly, breaking it.

"Kazu-**chan**, I think you were next," Mr. Yoshino told him. Customers streamed toward the shop, but Mr. Yoshino never forgot who was next in line.

His wife came out of the store and began to take customers' orders, too. "Well, if it isn't Kazu-chan!" She smiled. "Hello there!" Like her husband, Mrs. Yoshino had a head of completely white hair, but instead of tying a towel around it, she wore a white cloth folded in a crisp triangle.

"I hear those grades of yours are the best in the class," Mr. Yoshino said cheerfully and took the metal bowl from Kazuo's hand. "Your dad was bragging about you the other night. He said you're going to get into the engineering department of a national university!"

Kazuo pictured his father at Chujiya, the smoky bar by the station, bragging loudly. Father liked to tell jokes and watch TV with the family, but whenever he stopped for a drink after work, he came home loud and irritable. He would

The war World War II, lasting from 1939 to 1945. Almost all the nations of the world were involved. There were two groups fighting each other: the Allies (United States, England, and Soviet Union) and the Axis (Germany, Italy, and Japan). Atomic bombs dropped on Hiroshima and Nagasaki in August 1945 and large bombing attacks on Tokyo preceded the Japanese surrender in August 1945.

start lecturing Kazuo and his little brother Yasuo as they sat watching TV.

"I want you boys to study hard, you hear me? Your old man is working his tail off every day so you can get into good schools."

"The best grades in the class?" Mrs. Yoshino echoed. "Well, then, your father must be looking forward to your future!"

"I'm not sure they're the best . . ." Kazuo started to say.

It was true that Kazuo's grades were good. But he was hardly the top student in his class: section three of the fourth grade at West Ito Elementary School. The top student was probably Keiko Sasaki, who, like Kazuo, lived in company housing for the Nihon Optics factory.

"What are you going to be when you grow up, Kazu-chan?" Mr. Yoshino dipped his hand slowly into the water again.

"I don't know yet." Kazuo thought about how his father had grown up on a farm and wasn't able to go to high school when **the war** started. He had gone to vocational school instead. Then, at fifteen, he'd moved to Tokyo and started work at his current company as a factory hand.

"We're living in good times now, that's for sure," Mr. Yoshino said. "There's no war on, there's food to eat, and anybody who wants to study can study to his heart's content. During the war, there were air raids every day, and we had to worry about what we were going to eat before thinking about schoolwork. Can you imagine? Day in, day out, the first thing on our minds was where we'd get our next meal."

Every time an adult spoke this way, Kazuo felt lazy and useless. He often got wrapped up in TV and comic books and didn't study beyond what was absolutely necessary. What really mattered to him right now was figuring out how to run like Bob Hayes, the American who'd won the gold medal in the one-hundred-meter dash at the **Tokyo Olympics** last year. Watching him on TV—seeing him keep his muscular body low to the ground as he shot out of the starting blocks like a bullet—was something that Kazuo would never forget.

Tokyo Olympics

The Summer Olympics held in Tokyo in October 1964. For the Japanese, the Tokyo Olympics symbolized achieving international acceptance after World War II. The Tokyo Olympics were legendary in Japan for performances by American sprinter Robert "Bullet Bob" Hayes, the Ethiopian marathoner Abebe Bikila, and the Japanese women's volleyball team. Bob Hayes later became a wide receiver for the Dallas Cowboys American football team.

Ever since then, Kazuo and his classmate Nobuo, the son of the local butcher, had been going to an empty lot after school. They would crouch and try to charge into a sprint, just like Bob Hayes. But they often wound up stumbling, or, in trying not to stumble, coming up too soon.

"I wonder if this is just impossible for us Japanese," Nobuo had recently said in frustration.

"Why would it be impossible?" Kazuo asked.

"We're built differently, that's why," Nobuo said. "The final hundred-meter dash didn't have a single Japanese athlete in it. The runners were all tall black people and white people. None of them looked like us."

Kazuo had decided that Nobuo was right. It wasn't just the hundred-meter dash. Even in judo, a Japanese sport that had just become an Olympic event, the great Inokuma of Japan had lost in the finals to a Dutch athlete.

Japan had lost to America in World War II and to a European athlete at the 1964 Olympics, Kazuo realized. Maybe grown-ups were always telling children to study harder because that would finally make Japan come out on top. Thinking about it this way, Kazuo felt that adults were very selfish creatures.

Mr. Yoshino put a block of tofu into Kazuo's metal bowl. "You're still young, Kazu-chan," he was saying. "So it's not so simple to predict what you'll do down the road, is it?" The shop owner placed a thin piece of paper over the top of the bowl to keep the dust off.

"Anyway, the best thing you can do for your mom and pop is grow up healthy, so they won't have to worry," Mr. Yoshino added.

Then the tofu maker and his wife both smiled at Kazuo. He smiled and nodded back.

Several days later, a cold rain fell. Afterward, autumn seemed to come fully upon the town, filling it with cold air. In the midst of the chill, Mr. Yoshino's hand grew steadily redder. Kazuo could see it swelling up so that it looked like a soggy sweet bun. Even so, Mr. Yoshino's movements remained exactly the same. Slowly dipping his hand into the water, he carefully brought the tofu up from the bottom of the tank.

One afternoon in mid-October, Kazuo grabbed the metal bowl as always and headed over to Yoshino's Tofu. But the storefront was completely deserted. The door was closed; a white curtain hung inside, covering the window.

A sign was posted on the old wooden door. There were several characters that Kazuo couldn't read, but he could make out the words "today" and "closed" so he returned home.

In the kitchen his mother had begun to prepare dinner. Yasuo was sprawled in the living room, watching a TV show called *Shonen Jet*.

"**Okaasan**, the tofu store was closed today." Kazuo returned the metal bowl and ten yen to his mother.

"Really? I wonder if **Ojiisan** caught a cold," she said. "The weather turned chilly so suddenly." Then she added, "If you've got homework, Kazuo, finish it up before dinner."

"Okay," he said. He took out his *kanji*-writing notebook and pretended to study at the table. But his eyes were fixed on the TV screen.

Okaasan — Mother, mom, mommy. A very common variation of this is *Okaachan* or just *Kaachan*.

Ojiisan — Grandpa, or what you might call any elderly man whose name you do not know. *Ojiichan* is a less formal form of the word.

-san — *-San* is a suffix added to names to show respect. It is used for both men and women, and can be attached to either the family name or the personal name. For example, the person we call Mr. Tanaka is called "Tanaka-san" in Japan. If his personal name is Hiroshi, his friends may call him "Hiroshi-san." Japanese people almost always attach a suffix to a person's name (but not to their own).

Kanji — Japanese characters, or ideograms, originally developed in China. Japanese elementary schoolchildren must learn hundreds of *kanji* before they reach middle school. See also page 129.

The next day Kazuo raced home. He and Nobuo had spent a long time practicing running in the empty lot, and now he was late for his trip to the tofu maker's shop. His mother was already home from work.

Kazuo tossed his backpack into the living room and grabbed the metal bowl. "Okaasan, I'm going to the tofu store now," he called.

"Kazuo." His mother came toward him. "You don't have to go today."

"What? Why?" He stopped in his tracks.

"Ojiisan from the tofu store died yesterday. He had a stroke and collapsed. So starting today, you don't have to go anymore."

Not knowing how to respond, Kazuo exhaled softly. Then he slowly removed his shoes.

"Ha-ha! You forgot your job!" Yasuo teased Kazuo, turning on the TV. *Shonen Jet* appeared in black and white on the screen.

"**Niichan**, let's watch," Yasuo said. But Kazuo remained in the space where the entryway joined the living room, as if frozen.

At dinner, their father drank hot *sake* and ate stew without the usual tofu in it.

"So the man from the tofu store died, did he?" he said in a low voice.

"He was getting on in years," Mother said.

"He must have been the only tofu maker who still used well water and boiled the soymilk on a wood stove," said Father. "What's going to happen to his shop now?"

"There's no way his wife can run it by herself," Mother answered. "They say she's going to close it. Apparently they had a son, but he died during the war. He was in middle school."

Father looked surprised at that. "I saw the old man often at the bar, but he never said a word about a son."

"Yes, well, everyone in the neighborhood knew him as the nicest, smartest boy in the junior high. In early March 1945, there was an air raid. He had to be at a factory instead of school to support the war effort, and the factory was bombed. He never returned."

Kazuo suddenly remembered what Mr. Yoshino had said: that growing up healthy was the most important thing he could do. He pictured the tofu maker's red, swollen hand drawing out the tofu.

From now on, I'm going to remember to chew my tofu when I eat it, thought Kazuo. And I'm going to try to do my homework without my mom telling me to do it.

He felt bad that he'd never realized just how good Mr. Yoshino's tofu really was until now.

Niichan
Brother, used to address an older brother in a casual way. Adding "o" at the start of the word is more polite— *Oniichan.*

Sake
An alcoholic beverage made by fermenting rice. *Sake* (pronounced sah-kay) has a long history in Japan and is used in many rites and celebrations. It can be drunk warm or chilled.

Yasuo's Dog Dreams

Kazuo's family lived in the Nihon Optics company housing. Companies often built homes on land they owned, renting them out to their employees cheaply.

Kazuo could not really understand why a company would do this. According to his father, it had to do with tax strategy. Father often grumbled about it. "Figuring out ways to get more tax money out of people is the government's job."

But Kazuo's teacher, Mr. Honda, had explained taxes differently. He'd said that they were the reason that children got to go to school.

"Tax money is used for all sorts of things: teachers' salaries, this school building, even your textbooks."

That made Kazuo think taxes were a very good thing. Maybe there were good taxes and bad taxes, he decided.

Their neighborhood was encircled by a fence with a sign: Nihon Optics Company Housing. Each of the four complexes was a plain, one-story building made up of five identical housing units in a row.

When you opened the outer sliding door of Kazuo's house, there was a small entryway with a concrete floor, where everybody took off their shoes before coming inside. The entryway led to the living room, about the size of six **tatami** mats, with a low, round table in the center. There, Kazuo and his family ate their meals and watched TV. At night, they moved the table to a corner of the room, and Mother and Father laid out their bedding to sleep. The right side of the room opened into a closet that held bedding for the entire family, along with their summer and winter clothing packed in wooden boxes for ventilation. To the rear of the six-mat living room was a four-and-a-half-mat room—Kazuo and Yasuo's room. There was also a kitchen with two gas burners for cooking. The only bathroom was off the entryway. Naturally, there was no bathtub; every other day the family went to a public bathhouse called Fujita Yu in the center of the West Ito shopping area.

Kazuo had never thought of his house as small. After all, his buddies lived in small houses, too. Nobuo's had the family butcher shop on the first floor, and a space the size of Kazuo's house on the second. That was where Nobuo lived with his older brother, parents, and grandmother—five people altogether. When Nobuo came to play at Kazuo's, he would always say, "Wow, you've got your own desk and your

---

Tatami

Straw mats used as flooring. Traditional Japanese floors are not wooden or carpeted but are made up of straw mats called *tatami*. A *tatami* mat is about the size of a sleeping body, or 3 feet by 6 feet, and the size of a room is described by the number of mats that fit in it, usually 4½ or 6 mats. Nowadays, many Japanese homes have only one room with *tatami*, but in Tokyo in the 1960s, homes and apartments were more traditional and had mostly *tatami*-mat rooms.

own room, even if you have to share it with Yasuo."

Hearing this, Kazuo felt fortunate. But he also knew there were people in the world who lived in much bigger houses. Even in West Ito, there were houses up a slope in District 4 that in no way resembled the small company housing units strung together like cars in a freight train. Most of the District 4 houses were two stories high with yards or gardens. Kazuo figured daily life in houses like these must be just like in *Leave It to Beaver*, an American TV show he really liked.

The main character in *Leave It to Beaver* was a boy named Beaver because his two front teeth were big, like a beaver's. In Beaver's house, the mother and father had their own bedroom, and Beaver and his older brother each had their own bedroom, too. The family ate their meals in a dining room. They also had a living room with a large sofa and fireplace for sitting around talking and watching TV.

Whenever Kazuo walked through District 4, he couldn't help feeling a little envy. So he often repeated a pet phrase of his mother's: "If you're always looking for something better, you're never satisfied."

His little brother, Yasuo, also wished they could live in a home with a big yard and not in company housing. That was because Yasuo wanted a dog. But pets weren't allowed in company housing, where the most you could have was a fish in a tank, or a bird that stayed in a cage. Dogs barked, so they in particular were strictly forbidden. But Yasuo was always petting dogs he saw on the street.

Kazuo didn't really know why Yasuo liked dogs. Sometimes he thought it was because of TV shows such as **Lassie** and **The Littlest Hobo** and **The Adventures of Rin Tin Tin**. But even before last year, when his parents bought the family's first TV to watch the Olympics, Yasuo had liked dogs and would stare at picture books with dogs in them. Mother was always telling Yasuo not to go up to just any dog, because some might have rabies. "Rabies is a scary sickness, Yasuo. If a dog with rabies bites somebody, the person will begin to drool just like a dog and die in a fit of moaning."

Whenever Mother told him that, Yasuo would say, "Really?" with a slightly pale face. Then he'd avoid going up to dogs for the next two or three days. But soon he would forget about Mother's warning and go back to petting every dog he met.

Lassie

An American TV series about a loyal collie and his master, a boy. The show began in 1954 and lasted 19 years. Lassie was always rescuing people and solving problems. In Japanese cities, few homes were large enough to have a dog.

The Littlest Hobo

A Canadian TV series about a German shepherd that travels from town to town, helping people in need. At the end of each episode the dog would go off on his own. In the Canadian TV version (1963 to 1965), the dog did not have a name. In the Japanese version the dog was named London.

The Adventures of Rin Tin Tin

Another American TV series about a dog, this time a German shepherd. In the late 1800s, Rin Tin Tin and his owner, Rusty, were adopted by troops at a U.S. Cavalry Post called Fort Apache AZ. The show aired from 1954 to 1959 and was broadcast in Japan in the 1960s.

After Mr. Yoshino died, every day a man from a shop called Imamura Tofu came to sell tofu in the neighborhood just after five o'clock. That gave Kazuo a lot of time to work on his Bob Hayes training. Today, as usual, Kazuo headed to the empty lot with Nobuo after school. Yasuo used to wait in the schoolyard for them, but lately he had started going home by himself. Again there was no sign of him.

"Yasuo isn't a baby anymore," Nobuo told Kazuo.

"I don't care if he goes home on his own, but my mother gets all worried and says I should keep an eye on him."

When Kazuo and Nobuo reached the empty lot, they started on their running. Deep down, Kazuo knew that neither of them would ever be able to run like Bob Hayes, no matter how hard they tried. Both of them were starting to get a little tired of their project.

After four o'clock, it turned chilly. Soon, they were sucking in startlingly cold air as they practiced.

"Let's head home," Nobuo said.

"Yeah, let's go," Kazuo answered.

By the time Kazuo got home, it was starting to get dark. When he opened the front door, he could see Yasuo watching TV in the dim living room without the light on. Sitting on his knees, Yasuo was staring into the set at *Shonen Jet.* He looked up when Kazuo entered.

"Oh, Oniichan, you're back."

"Hey, Yasuo, at least turn on a light." Kazuo pulled the

string of the light fixture in the center of the room.

"Did you bring home your left-over bread from lunch?" Yasuo asked. Students who could not eat all of the bread in their school lunch had to take it home.

Shonen Jet

A Japanese TV action show for kids, broadcast in the early 1960s, featuring a boy detective named Jet and his dog, Shane, who fought against evil.

"Bread from lunch?" Kazuo said, sitting next to Yasuo. "Why are you asking me? You're the one who can never finish."

"Yeah, I know, but . . . " Yasuo pouted a bit, then gazed off.

Kazuo looked at his brother closely. "Hey, Yasuo, you're keeping something from me, aren't you?" He grabbed Yasuo in a headlock and squeezed his head. "Come on, out with it."

"Oww, stop it, that hurts! I'm not hiding anything!"

The front door opened. Mother was home. "What are you two doing?"

Kazuo quickly unwrapped his arms from Yasuo's head.

"You'll bother the neighbors!"

"Okaasan, Niichan's picking on me!" Yasuo whined. He ran to hide behind her.

"I'm not picking on you. You're the one who's keeping secrets."

"Kazuo!" Mother raised her voice again. "You're older, so you shouldn't pick on your brother, you understand? Now I want both of you to stop watching TV and finish your homework."

Kazuo stuck his lip out in a huff. "Come on! Why do I always have to be the one to get scolded? You and Dad always take Yasuo's side."

But there was no arguing with the stern expression on Mother's face. Kazuo turned off the TV. Then he took his books out of his bag and began to do his math homework.

The next day, after Kazuo went to the empty lot with Nobuo, he got home to find the house completely dark. The front door was still locked. He opened it and turned the lights on throughout the house. Yasuo was nowhere, and his school bag was missing as well.

"That idiot! Where on earth did he go?" Kazuo grew anxious, thinking both about Yasuo and what Mother would say. Wondering if he should alert a neighbor, he hurried to put his shoes back on. Just then the door opened. Yasuo's face appeared in the darkness, wearing a dejected expression.

"Yasuo, where the heck were you?"

"Niichan, I'm sorry." Yasuo stepped into the living room and slipped off his school bag. "I didn't go anywhere. I was just playing at my friend's house."

It was the time of day when *Shonen Jet* was starting, but Yasuo made no move to switch on the TV. Instead, he sat down glumly next to the table.

"Really?"

"Yeah, really."

Kazuo could tell that Yasuo was keeping something

from him again. But Yasuo looked so pitiful, Kazuo didn't have the heart to press him about it. He just reached over and turned on the TV himself.

Dinner that night was boiled flatfish, *miso* soup with the new tofu from Imamura's, and pickled vegetables—a very boring meal to Kazuo. He felt that dinner would be much more enjoyable if they were having croquettes or curry rice, to say nothing of the beefsteak and whole roasted turkey he saw on American TV shows. But if he said that, he was sure to get a lecture from his mother:

"Be grateful for what you have, Kazuo. If you're always looking for something better, you're never satisfied. You should be thankful that you get three square meals a day."

Kazuo kept his mouth shut and chewed. Now, he always forced himself to chew one bite of tofu before he swallowed the rest whole.

"By the way, Kazuo." Mother stopped eating for a moment. "I'm going to ask you only once. You haven't been playing in that big empty lot in Hara, have you?"

"The empty lot in Hara? You mean the one by the Haneto River?"

Mother nodded.

The Haneto was a river of sludge that separated West Ito from the town of Hara. Both of the river's banks were packed with small- and medium-sized factories that dumped their wastewater into it, so it always had a nasty smell.

Bedding

In traditional Japanese homes, people sleep on a *futon* laid out on the floor. A *futon* set consists of a bottom mattress (a thick cotton pad) and a top blanket (a bit like a comforter). To make the sleeping area usable during the day, the *futon* is stored on a shelf in a large closet until it is needed.

"I never go to that place. It's far away and it stinks, plus it's where all the kids from Hara Grade School hang out," Kazuo said.

"Really? In that case, there's no problem." Mother sounded relieved.

"Did something happen over there?" Father asked.

"I heard that there are some stray dogs living there. Apparently one of them bit a child, so tomorrow the public health department is sending the dog catchers in. They say it's better to stay away until the dogs are gone, so I thought I'd warn the boys." Mother picked up her chopsticks again.

Father nodded, his face slightly red from drinking beer. "I'll take some rice now," he told Mother.

She put some into his bowl.

Then the four of them finished their meal as if nothing had happened. Only Kazuo had noticed that when Mother brought up the subject of the Hara lot, Yasuo's body had stiffened, then trembled ever so slightly.

At nine o'clock, Kazuo and Yasuo said goodnight to their parents and crawled into their **bedding**. In the living room next door, they could hear the old-fashioned speech of actors in a period drama their parents were watching on TV.

"Yasuo, you awake?" Kazuo whispered.

Yasuo did not reply, but Kazuo could hear his breathing from inside his blanket.

"You went to the Hara lot today, didn't you?" Kazuo asked him.

"No," Yasuo said in a small voice.

"Liar." Kazuo poked his head from under his blanket and put it under Yasuo's. "I won't tell Mom and Dad, so out with it. What happened over there?"

"You really won't tell?" Yasuo said, sounding ready to cry.

"I won't tell. I promise." Kazuo stuck out his pinkie finger.

"You really won't, right?" Yasuo hooked his own pinkie around Kazuo's. He took a breath and then spoke. "I was feeding a dog over there."

"What? You mean the dog Mom was talking about at dinner, the one who bit somebody?"

"No, no, nothing like that! My dog is just a puppy. If somebody doesn't feed him, he'll die." Yasuo was almost sobbing as he explained that he had discovered the dog four days earlier. One afternoon he'd decided to go to Hara, where he and Kazuo normally never went. In the lot, he'd found a black puppy. He knew he couldn't keep a dog in company housing, so he'd been feeding the dog in secret.

"That's why you asked if I had any bread left from my lunch?" Kazuo said.

"Yeah . . . But you know what? Today I saved all of my bread and margarine from lunch again and went over there, but the lot had a wire fence around it. Somebody from the health department was there, and he said I couldn't go in. I was worried about the puppy, so I stayed around for a really long time, trying to see him."

Yasuo fell silent for a second.

"Do you think they'll catch that puppy tomorrow?" he whispered.

"Do you want to go and see for yourself?" Kazuo asked.

He felt Yasuo nod yes in the dark.

"Wait in the schoolyard till my last class is over. We'll go to Hara right after school."

"Really, Niichan?"

"Really. I'll go with you, no matter what. So let's get some sleep."

Kazuo took his head out from under Yasuo's blanket and burrowed back into his own. The place where he laid his head felt a little cold, but not as cold as when he had first crawled in for the night. It wasn't long before Yasuo fell fast asleep, drawing soft, even breaths.

Kazuo lay awake a while longer. He'd said, for Yasuo's sake, that he would go with him to the lot tomorrow. But he had absolutely no idea what to do about the puppy when they got there.

"Maybe I'll get an idea tomorrow," Kazuo murmured as he closed his eyes.

The next day Yasuo was in a corner of the playground, hanging from the iron high-bar as he waited for his brother.

"All right, Yasuo, let's go," Kazuo said. The two of them exchanged few words as they walked briskly toward the lot at Hara. It took a good twenty minutes to get there, and today those twenty minutes seemed even longer to Kazuo. He was still worried about what to do.

Finally, they saw the Haneto River. Usually, they plugged their noses and howled, "Pew, it stinks!" But today they both said nothing as they crossed the concrete bridge and rushed toward the empty lot.

The dog-catching operation was already underway. The lot, more like a small field, was surrounded by people who were watching, as if it were a show. Kazuo and Yasuo pushed their way through the crowd, finally finding a spot in the front row.

In the tall, wilted grass, dog catchers were running around with big nets and poles that had wire hoops on the ends. "Over there!" they shouted. "No, over here!"

"Have they caught any dogs yet?" Kazuo asked a man wearing a cook's uniform.

Truck with cage and sign: "Animal control in progress. Please go around."

"They got several already. Look, they're in that truck over there." The man pointed to a truck parked at the side of the road. A large cage covered in wire mesh sat on the freight platform in the back.

"Is the puppy in there?" Kazuo asked Yasuo.

His little brother hurried over to the truck to check. He returned a minute later.

"He's not in there," he whispered, sounding relieved.

Kazuo glanced back at the lot. That meant that the dog the catchers were now trying to capture might be Yasuo's puppy. Again Kazuo wondered what to do. If one was the puppy, he could try begging them to let it go. Or he could act like a TV hero and undo the lock on the cage, setting all the dogs free.

He kept his eyes glued to the dog catchers running around in the tall grass. "Right there!" a man yelled, and then the dog catchers began to close in on a particular spot. The high-pitched yips of a dog came from the center of the circle they had made.

A round of applause rose from the onlookers.

As the applause continued, a light-brown dog was led from the lot, yanked along by a dog catcher. The dog's eyes were wide open with fright, his tail tucked between his legs.

"Is that the dog?" Kazuo murmured.

Yasuo shook his head no.

The dog stiffened its legs to resist being pulled forward any further. But there was no way the poor animal could escape with the wire collar around his neck. The dog catcher continued dragging him over to the cage and then threw him inside.

After that, the wire fencing around the edge of the lot was taken down, and the spectators began to disperse little by little.

Kazuo and Yasuo stayed right where they were until the truck finally left the lot.

"I'm glad the little puppy didn't get caught," Yasuo murmured. "But I feel bad for that other dog."

Kazuo thought of the stray dog being dragged along by a wire ring around his neck and forced into the cage on the truck. "Yeah, I feel bad, too," he said. Then he put an arm around Yasuo's shoulders. "Maybe someone found the puppy and is taking care of him right now at home."

"I sure hope so," said Yasuo.

"Hey, maybe we can adopt a dog when we're older," Kazuo said.

"Yeah, that would be great. What should we call him?" Yasuo asked.

"Let's think of some names," Kazuo suggested. He rattled off every single name he could think of as they slowly walked home, the cold air nipping at their necks.

Milk

Every day at about eleven forty-five, just over halfway through fourth period, everyone in Kazuo's classroom began to grow restless.

That was because their attention would shift to the smells drifting down the hall from the large room where their lunches were being made. They would forget about their studies as they tried to guess what the day's meal might be. They had, of course, received a menu from the teacher at the beginning of the month. It was printed on cheap brown paper and was also posted at the back of the classroom. But nobody ever actually looked at that sheet. The reason was that looking at the monthly menu took half the fun out of eating lunch. Everybody knew that imagining what was for lunch, based on the smells drifting in from the kitchen—just when everyone was beginning to feel hungry—was the first step in enjoying the school lunch.

Kazuo felt strongly that school lunch was a very big deal. The school lunch program had started after the war so that everybody, even children from poor families, could eat at school. Every day from Monday through Friday, everyone—from students to teachers to the principal—ate exactly the same thing.

> **Hijiki**
> A brown sea vegetable that grows wild on rocky coastlines. It has been part of a balanced diet in Japan for centuries. Most Japanese mothers want their kids to eat it, but most kids hate it, kind of how American kids feel about spinach.

One morning, as Mr. Honda explained how to multiply numbers with two digits, Kazuo only pretended to study the blackboard. He was trying with all his might to identify the day's main dish.

Typically, if the smell was curry, everyone would smile. That meant the day's menu was curry stew. All the children would suddenly become diligent students, their pencils scribbling twice as fast in their notebooks so they could eat sooner. At lunchtime, even children who never asked for seconds would jostle for a spot in line to get another helping.

On the other hand, if the hallway smelled strongly of soy sauce, gloom would instantly descend. A strong soy sauce smell meant that the meal was boiled *hijiki* seaweed and vegetables, which didn't have a single fan among the students, including Kazuo.

But most of the time, Kazuo thought the food in school lunch was delicious. And because of school lunch, he got to discover foods he had never tasted before—even foods from American TV shows. For example, he had seen spaghetti on the comedy program *The Three Stooges*, which always featured three men raising a ruckus with foolish antics. At first, Kazuo had not known the dish was called "spaghetti." He'd

Udon

A thick, white, wheat noodle (similar to spaghetti) usually served in a big bowl of broth with scallions, tempura, or other ingredients. In western Japan the broth is made from light soy sauce; in eastern Japan the broth is dark brown. *Udon* is a very popular lunchtime dish because it is quick to prepare and inexpensive.

Soba

A thin, beige-colored buckwheat noodle. It is served chilled with a dipping sauce or in hot broth as a noodle soup. *Soba* is served at cheap lunchtime counters and at fancy restaurants, and it is easily made at home for a quick meal or snack. It is also a traditional New Year's Eve dish.

only known that noodles piled on a dish were eaten laboriously with a fork by a guy named Curly, who was a big blockhead.

So in the spring of his second-grade year, when a mass of fat noodles, thinner than **udon** yet thicker than **soba**, were served to Kazuo on his metal school lunch plate, he was excited. He was going to eat the same food as blockheaded Curly! Kazuo had poked Nobuo in the seat next to him and asked if he knew the name of the odd-looking noodles with red sauce.

"Spaghetti, of course!" Nobuo had flared his nostrils and grinned confidently. "You should know better than to ask that question of a butcher's son."

Kazuo wasn't sure how being a butcher's son related to spaghetti, but he was impressed that Nobuo knew the name of this foreign food.

Still, school lunch had one flaw. The name of that flaw, which was enough to bring disgusted looks to students' faces when they said it, was **miruku**.

Miruku, or "milk," referred to a certain lukewarm, white liquid passed out in metal cups to everyone. The substance was nothing at all like cow's milk, commonly known in Japanese as *gyunyu*. This other drink was so unlike *gyunyu* that it had to have its own name—a name reserved for powdered skim milk.

Just how disgusting was it? First, Kazuo had decided that it gave off exactly the same foul smell as a kitchen drain. Second, when he managed to take a drink despite the smell, a very strange sweet and sour taste filled his mouth. If he left his *miruku* until the end of the meal, with the plan to swallow it all in one big gulp, it would congeal completely and taste exactly like melted butter mixed with water.

Unfortunately, Kazuo's previous teacher, Mr. Tanaka, had flown into a terrifying rage the year before, yelling at the class one day when they'd refused to drink the *miruku*.

> **Miruku**
>
> Japanese pronunciation of "milk," used to mean a type of powdered skim milk. In the old days, the Japanese rarely ate dairy products. Many Japanese still have trouble digesting them. Traditional Japanese cooking does not use cheese, milk, cream sauces, or butter. Until the 1960s, the Japanese considered milk a kind of health food or medicine.

Middle school students drinking their *miruku*.

"All of you are spoiled rotten! When the war was on, people on the battlefield had to drink mud to quench their thirst. If you can't drink a cup or two of this milk, what does that make you? All of you, drink! Until everyone drinks, no one leaves this classroom for lunch recess!"

Frightened by Mr. Tanaka's outburst, Kazuo and his classmates had taken their cups of *miruku* back to their seats and somehow forced it down.

And for the rest of the year, the *miruku* had to be drunk. Kazuo and the other boys in his class had begun to hold contests to see who could drink the most. After they'd eaten the food, they had dared each other to drink as much as possible of the completely cooled, leftover *miruku* to demonstrate fortitude. The game was put to an end when Yukichi Nakajima, the class tough guy, drank four cups of *miruku* and then had an upset stomach for a week.

After Mr. Honda became their teacher at the beginning of fourth grade, Kazuo's class no longer had to drink all of their *miruku*. Mr. Honda was a man of about thirty who never raised his voice. During their first lunch period as fourth-graders, after everyone had said "**Itadakimasu**" at the start of the meal, Mr. Honda had told them, "Everyone, before you eat, please watch me."

Mr. Honda brought his cup of *miruku* to his mouth and, holding his nose, gulped it down. When he finished, he laughed and said, "Wow, that was disgusting!"

Everyone in the class, including Kazuo, laughed heartily. With a single phrase, Mr. Honda had broken the spell cast by Mr. Tanaka.

"No one, including myself, likes the taste of *miruku*," Mr. Honda said quietly. "This is not milk. And this kind of powdered skim milk is completely different from what you would find in a store. It is nothing but the sediment left over from making butter, which has been dissolved in hot water. In the United States, this kind of powdered skim milk is actually fed to cows."

"Fed to cows!" the class cried.

Itadakimasu
Japanese expression used before eating, meaning "I humbly receive." It expresses gratitude toward the people who bring us our food such as farmers, ranchers, fishermen, delivery people, grocers, cooks, etc. It is also a way of giving thanks to the elements (water, sun, earth, air) that grow our food and to the plants, fish, and animals that give their lives so that we may eat.

"Settle down, everyone." Mr. Honda held up a hand. "Our fifth period class is social studies, so after lunch, I will talk with you about why something that is used as feed for American cattle is being given to us for lunch. But now, about this *miruku*. Those of you who can drink it, please do so. But if you cannot drink it, please do not force yourself. As your teacher, I will not scold you if you leave it in your cup. I do ask, however, that you remember the lunch ladies who worked hard to prepare it for you. If you choose to leave it, please say a silent word of apology to them before doing so."

Everyone obediently nodded.

And after lunch recess, Mr. Honda explained further. He told the children that Japan had been faced with a serious food shortage after World War II. Many Japanese children were suffering from malnutrition. So large quantities of canned fish and powdered milk had been donated, and *miruku* became part of a new school lunch program. It was a desperate time, and even feed for cattle was accepted with gratitude.

But twenty years had passed since the end of the war, thought Kazuo. The Olympics had even been held in Tokyo, and Japan was economically better off than before. So why was *miruku* still being served? The reason was that Japan had signed an agreement with the United States. It promised that American soldiers could be stationed inside Japan, and in return, if Japan were attacked by another country, America would defend Japan. As payment for this alliance with the U.S., Japanese elementary school children had to drink "powdered skim milk" every day.

After hearing Mr. Honda's lesson, Kazuo was very upset. He felt the situation was completely unfair.

That evening at dinnertime, Kazuo told his parents and Yasuo what he had learned.

His parents reacted much less strongly than he had expected.

His mother tamped his father's rice into a bowl. As always, she said, "During the war and afterward, people had nothing to eat at all. We're lucky to have what we have."

His father, whose face was red again from drinking beer, said, "I wonder if Mr. Honda is a Communist," and brought a bite of rice to his mouth.

Yasuo was the only one to agree with Kazuo. "I hate that awful *miruku*. The smell of it alone makes me want to throw up. If that agreement with America ever goes away, maybe *miruku* will go away, too."

But Kazuo did not think that the agreement would

disappear anytime soon. So he tried to teach himself to forget about the *miruku* that always accompanied the school lunch.

Today, what he detected in the smells wafting through the hallway was soy sauce fried in oil.

Tatsuta-style fried whale, he thought.

Whale was the meat that was served most often in school lunches. Deep fried whale, whale cutlets, boiled whale. Kazuo would have preferred chicken and pork, or beef, but the budget for school lunch rarely allowed for that.

Even Nobuo, the son of a butcher, said he had never eaten beefsteak. And he ate chicken and pork so few times each month that he could count them on his fingers.

Tatsuta-style

A style of breaded, deep-fried meat such as whale, pork, chicken, or mackerel. After marinating in soy sauce and mirin, the meat is sprinkled with *katakuri-ko* (potato starch) or corn starch before frying. At McDonald's in Japan you can sometimes find a "Tatsuta-style chicken burger" on the menu.

Whale

Whales have been eaten in Japan since ancient times, and the Japanese have also used whale oil, bones, and whiskers for tools and for arts and crafts. In the 1950s and '60s, whale meat was served in school lunches because it had protein and cost less than other meats. Eating whale meat is no longer so popular in Japan, and Japanese whale hunts are regularly criticized by animal rights groups.

Today's food was placed on Kazuo's metal tray by a classmate on lunch duty, a boy wearing a white apron. It was, just as he had detected, whale meat in a thick breading. Next to the whale meat was bread, and next to that was the *miruku*.

"*Itadakimasu.*" A student leader said the word of thanks, and the class repeated it. Kazuo held his nose, just as Mr. Honda had done, and downed his tepid *miruku* to get it over with. Then, sighing with relief, he looked down at the piece of fried whale. He could tell that it would be as tough as the sole of a shoe, as usual.

Still, Kazuo put the meat in his mouth and chewed laboriously. He couldn't help but think about how tender and delicious real beefsteak must be.

NOVEMBER

Children enjoying their school lunch.

Bathing and the Beatles

Kazuo's house didn't have a bathtub, so every other day his family went to the Fujita Yu **bathhouse**. Kazuo figured that fewer than half of the students in his class had bathtubs at home. Because demand was so high, West Ito also had two other public bathhouses, but of all three public baths, Kazuo liked Fujita Yu the best.

First of all, it had a much grander entrance than the other two, with a tile roof that sloped down on both sides to make an inverted U, like the roof of an old temple.

The next good thing about Fujita Yu was that it had a garden, complete with a pond where colorful carp swam. In the summer, there was no better way to cool off after a steaming hot bath than to sit out on the porch by the pond.

But the absolute best thing about Fujita Yu was its mural of Mount Fuji, which was huge compared with the murals in the other two bathhouses. The mountain's snow-covered summit soared to the ceiling at the center of the wall that separated the men's and women's baths. The fields beneath it

Bathhouse

A public bath, usually in a spacious building with a prominent chimney. Men and women bathe in separate large rooms. Each has rows of faucets and stools and one or two large tubs for soaking. Many people go to the bathhouse a couple times a week just to visit with neighbors. See also page 157.

Mount Fuji

The highest mountain in Japan, at 12,389 feet (3,776 meters). Mount Fuji is just west of Tokyo and can be seen from there on a clear day. The cone of Mount Fuji has become a symbol of Japan. Japanese bathhouses often have a big mural of a nature scene like Mount Fuji on the wall, to make you feel you are viewing it outside from a hot spring. Mount Fuji last erupted in 1707–8.

extended all the way to waves painted right where the main bathtubs met the wall. When you looked at the mural while submerged to your shoulders in hot water, you almost felt you'd come to a hot spring near **Mount Fuji** itself and were bathing as you gazed at it! Although Kazuo dreamed about living in a huge house like the ones on the hill in District 4, he couldn't help but feel that bathing at a public bath would always be more fun than bathing at home.

His family usually went to the bath shortly after eight p.m., after dinner. Kazuo enjoyed going earlier, when there weren't as many people in the main tub. Then you could stretch out your legs and arms as much as you wanted, and maybe even sneak in a swim when the lady supervisor wasn't looking. But Kazuo's family almost never bathed in the afternoons in autumn and winter. If you went in too early, you might catch a cold before bed.

In November, as the year started to draw to a close, Father's work at the Nihon Optics factory began to get busy. His job was to produce lenses used in making electronic equipment. Kazuo did not understand why you needed a lens for this, but according to Father, the lens was an important tool for making circuit boards. Lately, he had been working extra hours.

One night, Mother told Kazuo and Yasuo to go ahead to the bathhouse. The cartoon show they were watching, **Jungle Emperor,** had just ended. "Father is working late again," she explained.

> **Jungle Emperor**
>
> A popular Japanese TV animation series created by Osamu Tezuka, a Japanese manga artist and animator (and medical doctor!). From 1966 to 1967 NBC broadcast it in the U.S. under the title *Kimba the White Lion.* Many people have pointed out how the story, situation, and characters in the Disney movie *The Lion King* resemble those of *Kimba the White Lion.*

"We can go now, but when are *you* going to go?" Kazuo asked, switching off the TV.

"I imagine your father will be back before nine. I'll wait for him to eat his dinner and then we'll go together," Mother said. She handed them basins containing towels, soap, and a change of clothes. Then she gave thirty yen to Kazuo to pay the bathhouse fee.

"Take care you don't drop it. Okay, boys?"

Mother faced them to begin the list of warnings that she always gave them when they went to the bathhouse by themselves. "Absolutely no running. No horsing around in the water and disturbing the other people. No going into the deep tub reserved for the adults. Be sure you get into the tub all the way up to your shoulders and count to a hundred. When you're done, dry yourselves off properly and get right back into your clothes. Then come straight home without

Good Golly Gourd Island

A Japanese TV puppet drama (Japanese title: *Hyokkori Hyotan-jima*). Seven kids go on a picnic with their female teacher to Gourd Island. But the volcano suddenly explodes and the island starts drifting into the sea. The kids, their teacher, and other characters have various adventures. A boy called "Dr." and the sweet lion character Lion-kun have been favorites among Japanese kids.

dawdling. Don't go anyplace else. Don't walk down dark and deserted streets. . . . "

As usual, Kazuo and Yasuo pretended to listen, nodding impatiently. Then, finally, she was finished, and they could go.

Tonight, there was no wind, but the November night air felt chilly. Leaving company housing, they began to walk down the broad avenue that led to the shopping area.

Suddenly, Yasuo leaned toward Kazuo. "Niichan, did you bring it?"

"You bet I did." Kazuo reached into the pocket of his shorts and pulled out a small vinyl object in the shape of a gourd.

"All *right!*" Yasuo squealed when he saw it.

It was a model of an island, the setting of a TV puppet show called **Good Golly Gourd Island**. The show was broadcast Monday through Friday at five forty-five in the evening.

Gourd Island was home to a group of students who had traveled there on a field trip and ended up staying when the island began to drift around the world's oceans. The students-turned-islanders met pirates and good-hearted gunmen, and had to unravel mysteries and solve tough problems. The model that Kazuo gripped featured all of the characters from the TV series, each one about the size of a bean.

What Yasuo had in mind was to float the model in the

tub at the bathhouse and swim around
it, pretending to be the different characters. Yasuo, the animal lover, was a

Dad, Daddy. A less formal form is *Otohchan*.

Otohsan

huge fan of a lion called Lion-kun. Kazuo, like many other
boys his age at school, preferred the gunman called Dandy.

After they entered the shopping area, Kazuo and Yasuo
did not go directly to Fujita Yu. Instead, they stopped off
at Takahashi Meats, where Nobuo lived. Nobuo's father was
closing the butcher shop for the night, sorting meat and croquettes inside the glass cases.

"Good evening, sir." Yasuo spoke up first.

"Well, if it isn't Kazu-chan and Yasu-chan. Headed to
the bathhouse, are you?" Nobuo's father smiled at them from
over the counter.

Yasuo started chattering away. "**Otohsan** is going to
be late today because he has to work extra, so we're going
to the bathhouse by ourselves. Okaasan is waiting at home
for Otohsan. Then they're going to the bathhouse too. But
we're—"

Kazuo pushed in front of Yasuo to stop him from talking. "By the way, sir, is Nobuo-kun home? Since it's just Yasuo and me going to the bathhouse today, we wondered if he
wanted to go with us."

"I don't know about that kid. He hates bathing and just
went yesterday, so I'm not sure. But I'll ask him."

"Nobuo!" His father shouted up to the second floor.
"Kazu-chan and Yasu-chan came to see if you want to go to
the bathhouse."

Kazuo could hear the raucous sound of an electric guitar

upstairs. It was playing a popular English-language song.

Nobuo came bounding down the stairs. "Hey, Kazuo, Yasuo. Headed to the bathhouse, huh?"

"How about it, Nobuo, want to come?"

"Umm . . ." Nobuo gestured down at his legs. "I already put my pajamas on."

"Son, these boys came all the way over here to pick you up. Are you going to turn down their invitation?" Nobuo's father said. "Here, I'll give you some money. You three can have some sodas after your bath." Nobuo's father took a fifty-yen coin from a change basket.

"And Nobuo," he continued, "tell Haruo to quit listening to that ridiculous music for once and go with you." Haruo was Nobuo's older brother, who was in his second year of middle school.

Nobuo nodded and ran up the stairs.

In a few moments, the music stopped, and Nobuo came back down with a basin in his hands. Behind him was his older brother, Haruo, who was pimply with a close-shaven head and a sullen look on his face. He was carrying a basin, too.

His father frowned. "Haruo," he said sternly. "You're not going to spend your night listening to that silly record, you understand me? I want you to go straight to the bath, come home, study, and then get to bed early."

"It's not a silly record—it's **the Beatles**," Haruo said quickly, averting his eyes.

"What did you say? I've had enough of your talking back!" Nobuo's father smacked Haruo on the head with the palm of his hand. "I buy you a record player because you tell me you're going to study English. Then you stop helping at the store and spend every waking moment listening to those ridiculous songs. Get to the bathhouse, will you, and clear your head of that garbage!"

> **"Rock and Roll Music"**
> A song by famous American guitarist Chuck Berry and performed by the Beatles on their album *Beatles for Sale* (1964). Berry helped invent the style of what came to be known as rock 'n' roll music. This song celebrates the music that young people all over the world, including Japan, were listening to.

"I'm going. I'm going." Muttering and rubbing his head where his father had smacked him, Haruo left the store. The three younger boys followed.

Outside, Nobuo whispered in Kazuo's ear that Haruo had gone completely nuts over the Beatles, playing their songs over and over, day after day.

Kazuo knew that the Beatles were an American or British music group—four men with long hair. He also knew from the TV news that they would be coming to Japan the following year. But Kazuo had no idea why these four men were so popular among high school and middle school students.

Up ahead, Haruo was walking down the street with one hand stuck in his pants pocket as he sang something like *"Rok-kin roru myu-jik."* Kazuo guessed that was a Beatles song, too, maybe a hit song called **"Rock and Roll Music."**

Soon, they saw the entrance to Fujita Yu.

Haruo continued to croon strange words as the boys

passed under the half-curtain at the bathhouse entrance. Inside were separate doors to the men's bath and the women's, each flanked by a wall of shoe lockers that had large, wooden keys.

The boys found a spot in the entryway for their shoes. Stepping out of them, they slid open the door made of fogged glass and entered the men's side.

Just inside the doorway to the changing room was a tall counter where the woman who ran Fujita Yu sat to supervise the bathing areas.

"Well, if it isn't a small army!" she said to the four boys. Her round face broke into a smile.

"Yeah, I got stuck watching these babies." Haruo stopped singing and put his money on the counter.

"I'm not a baby, Niichan, and you know it," Nobuo said testily.

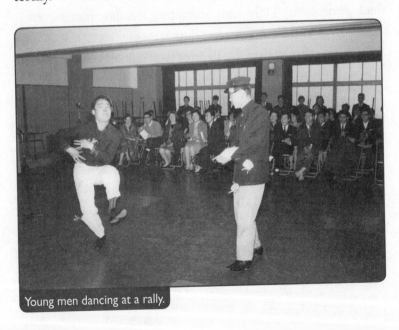

Young men dancing at a rally.

"You are so a baby. People who wet the bed at night are babies. There's just no other word for them."

"I did not wet the bed, you jerk." Nobuo turned bright red and tried to kick Haruo's leg.

"Oh yes, you did, just last week. That makes you a baby." Haruo easily dodged Nobuo's foot.

"All right, that's enough quarreling," said the supervisor.

"*Oi*, Haruo." Just then a voice called to Haruo from the corner of the changing room. Three middle-school boys with shaven heads, Haruo's classmates, stood there, completely naked.

> **Oi**
> "Hey!" or "Hey you!" An attention-getting word used by boys and men among close friends. It is very informal and a bit rough.

"Well, as proof that you're not babies, my babysitting duty ends here. Have a nice bath." Haruo headed toward his classmates while once again singing, "*Rok-kin roru myu-jik.*"

Nobuo made a nasty face in Haruo's direction. "Moron. When I get home, I'm telling my dad what he said."

"Well, they say siblings who fight are the close ones, but my goodness!" The supervisor laughed. "Okay, boys, that'll be fifteen yen for each of you."

"Two, please." Kazuo handed thirty yen for himself and Yasuo to the supervisor.

"Thank you very much. By the way, where are your mother and father today?" she asked.

Yasuo told her about their parents having to come later. "So we came all by ourselves," he explained.

"Did you really?" the supervisor said with a laugh. "Well, have a nice hot bath!"

"One, please," Nobuo said next, holding out the fifty-yen coin he had received from his father. "And after our bath we would like three sodas."

"No soda for your brother?" the supervisor asked.

"Big boys in middle school don't drink soda like us babies," Nobuo muttered grumpily.

The three boys found some baskets in the stack at the side of the changing area and put their clothes inside. This was the time of day when the bathhouse became the busiest. Both the tubs and the rows of faucets were crowded. Before heading to the tubs, Kazuo, Nobuo, and Yasuo hunted for an open faucet and sat down in front of it. They alternated running hot and cold water into basins until the water was just the right temperature to rinse off with. Then they rubbed soap on their towels and began scrubbing themselves clean. It was a bathhouse rule that you had to wash off completely before you got into the tubs.

Kazuo had learned that there were a lot of other unwritten rules. For example, if the water in the tub was a little too hot, you had to put up with it rather than add cold water to cool it down. When you washed at one of the faucets, you had to rinse all of your soap bubbles off the tiles so the next person could wash in a clean place. When you left the bath, you had to dry off completely to avoid dripping on the floor in the changing area. Et cetera, et cetera. If a child ever failed to follow one of these rules, an adult would surely correct him.

While Kazuo, Nobuo, and Yasuo were washing off, Haruo and his classmates came into the bathing area, all of them singing. The tune had changed from the one Haruo had been singing before, to something like "*Ee-tsu bina hahdo deizu naito*"—a song called "**A Hard Day's Night**."

A hit Beatles song (1964), featured in both a film and an album of the same name.

"A Hard Day's Night"

"Hey, is that a Beatles song, too?" Kazuo asked Nobuo, whose body was covered in suds.

"Probably." Nobuo kept scrubbing, showing no interest in the older boys' song.

"It sounds a little better than the tune he was singing before, don't you think?" Kazuo asked, looking over at Haruo and his friends.

"It just sounds that way because the bathhouse echoes," Nobuo replied.

Nobuo had a point: in the bathhouse, people's voices and the sounds of bathing bounced off the high ceiling and sounded much louder than they actually were.

Kazuo, Nobuo, and Yasuo got into a circle and washed each other's backs. Then they washed their heads off with soap and headed to the tub.

There were two tubs in the bathing area. The large one was not very deep, and the water was not very hot, so both children and adults could use it. But the smaller tub was for adults only. It was deeper, and the water was very hot. There were already six adults and four children in the bigger tub, leaving barely enough room for the three boys to squeeze in. But there were just two people using the adults' tub, leaving more than enough space for three boys.

"Oniichan, can we still play Gourd Island?" Yasuo asked, seeing the crowded main tub and blinking his eyes.

With this many people in the tub, it would be hard just

to get into the water, never mind float the model of Gourd Island and swim around it, Kazuo thought. But he couldn't say that to Yasuo, who was looking a little sad.

"You wait here," Kazuo told him. Ignoring Mother's earlier warning, he sat down on the edge of the adults' tub. Gingerly, he dipped his right toe in the water. He wanted to check exactly how deep it was.

The water was hot—very hot. Steeling himself against the heat, Kazuo reached his foot down and felt the bumpy tiles underneath. By then, his entire body was in the water. It went right up to his shoulders. The water would definitely be over Yasuo's head.

Kazuo carefully lifted himself out of the steaming bath and went over to Yasuo. His little brother was clutching the model of Gourd Island protectively to his chest.

"Yasuo, it's not going to work today. Like Okaasan said, the adults' pool is too deep for you, and the regular tub is too crowded. We're not supposed to bother other people, remember?"

Yasuo stuck out his lip, but nodded reluctantly.

Once the three boys got into the main tub, they folded their legs and sat, feeling cramped. The water was warm, and beads of sweat soon appeared on their foreheads.

"Lion-kun," Yasuo spoke to the bean-sized version of Lion-kun on the model of Gourd Island. "It looks like today won't work after all." The drifting island bobbed up and down near Yasuo's neck.

Nobuo darted a glance at Haruo and his classmates. "My brother and his friends sure are making a racket." They were hanging around near the end of a row of faucets and still singing *"Ee-tsu bina hahdo deizu naito."*

Kazuo had thought the song was cool at first. But hearing the same phrase over and over again was starting to drive him a little crazy.

"Is your brother this way at home, too?"

"Yeah, plus at home he plays his records, so I can't even watch TV in peace," Nobuo said. "I'm definitely telling my dad."

> **Tattoo**
>
> Japanese traditional tattoos are colorful images of geisha, dragons, or various mythological gods. The tattoos often cover the chest, back, and upper arms, and are usually not visible when the person is wearing regular street clothes, so sometimes the only place to see the tattoos is at a public bathhouse. (Many bathhouses used to forbid entry to anyone with tattoos.)

If they keep this up, they're going to get in trouble with the supervisor, Kazuo thought.

Just then he heard a loud splash.

The voices that had been repeating *"Ee-tsu bina hahdo deizu naito"* like a broken record suddenly stopped.

"Hey! That water's freezing!" Haruo yelled. The eyes of every single person in the bathhouse suddenly focused on him.

"What's that, little boy? The water felt cold?"

That was not the voice of the supervisor.

Through the steam, Kazuo could see bright colors moving closer. He focused his eyes. The colors belonged to a tattoo. It was a big **tattoo** of a blue dragon, the kind that gangsters had across their entire back or chest. Maybe Kazuo was going light-headed in the thick steam, but the vivid blue dragon seemed to be widening its eyes and opening its red mouth, about to sink its teeth into Haruo and his friends. A

Yakuza

Japanese mobsters, members of organized criminal gangs, traditionally involved in stolen goods, gambling, and loan sharking (loaning money at very high interest rates). There are many movies about *yakuza* in Japan; sometimes they are portrayed as folk heroes, similar to outlaws in American western movies. They often wear traditional tattoos.

long, thin, forked tongue stuck menacingly out of its mouth.

"You got some kind of problem with that?" Every time the dragon yelled, its blue body bulged, and its bright red mouth opened even wider.

Kazuo was transfixed by the combination of vivid blue and deep red. The tattoo belonged to Sabu-san, a young *yakuza*, or gangster. Everyone knew he and his buddies operated out of an office near the bars by the station, so the neighborhood was his "turf."

"You're the butcher's kid, aren't you?" Holding an empty plastic tub, Sabu-san stood squarely facing Haruo, glaring at him. Kazuo now realized that the gangster had thrown cold water on Haruo and his friends.

"Your old man works hard and sweats with all he's got," Sabu-san went on, "while you go around hollering in the bathhouse, bothering other people. What's wrong with you?"

By now Haruo had also realized who had thrown the water. He grew as meek as a kitten as Sabu-san yelled and banged the plastic tub against his thigh. Every time the tub hit his leg, it made a hollow sound, like a small drum.

Sabu-san's lecture went on for several minutes, and during that time, instead of *"Ee-tsu bina hahdo deizu naito,"* Haruo and his friends were forced to repeat, "Sorry. We're sorry," over and over.

After drinking the sodas paid for by Nobuo's father and leaving the bathhouse, Kazuo, Nobuo, and Yasuo walked back through the shopping area. The stores were closing one after another.

Nobuo flared his nostrils and hummed as he walked.

"Nobuo, you seem downright thrilled," Kazuo teased.

"You bet I'm thrilled! My stupid brother had it coming, telling all those lies about me wetting the bed. That's why he got it from old Sabu-san."

Nobuo had obviously been mortified by Haruo's teasing. Maybe that was because the story was true, Kazuo thought. He kept this thought to himself as the night air cooled his flushed cheeks.

Yasuo, walking at Kazuo's side, was speaking to Lion-kun on the model of Gourd Island again. "Looks like Okaasan was right, Lion-kun. In the bathhouse, you can't go around bothering other people. A lot of people use the bathhouse."

Kazuo listened to his little brother with a smile. Tonight had reminded him of something: all different kinds of people went to the bathhouse to wash up and soak in the hot water. There were children, students, company workers, people who worked at stores, and even *yakuza* like Sabu-san. Policemen and thieves probably got into the same tub and sat right next to each other sometimes without even knowing it. In the bathhouse, where everyone was naked, everyone was equal. And that, Kazuo thought, is why it feels so good to bathe at the bathhouse.

J-Boys

That November Kazuo made two new friends.

One was a tall, sturdily built boy named Minoru Kaneda, and the other was Minoru's physical opposite, a skinny boy named Akira Nishino. Kazuo got to be friends with Minoru and Akira after being assigned to the same small group for a class project. Also in the group was Keiko Sasaki, who lived in company housing just like Kazuo. Keiko was the group leader, and Kazuo was the assistant leader.

Nobuo was disappointed that he did not get to be in the same group as Kazuo. But he was glad to make two new friends too.

MINORU AND THE SCRAP CART

Five months earlier, on a Saturday in June, something had happened to make Kazuo want to be friends with Minoru. Kazuo had spent the afternoon rambling through the streets of West Ito, doing nothing in particular, and had ended up on top of the hill in District 4. There had been days and days of gloomy rain, and he was staring at the big houses with yards, watching the town below him gradually light up in the sunshine. Whenever he stood here, looking out from this height, Kazuo felt like a bird soaring through the sky. Sometimes he would pick out different tiny roofs in the town and imagine what kind of people lived underneath them and what they might be doing.

Kazuo felt a thin layer of sweat form on his forehead. The June sunlight was growing stronger. He closed his eyes against it, and behind his eyelids, the light seemed to gather various sounds: people's voices and footfalls, car engines, the rustling of leaves. . . .

Chirin, chirin.

Somewhere in the mixture of sounds, he heard the faint ringing of a bell.

Kazuo opened his eyes. It was a brass bell from a two-wheeled cart piled high with bundles of old newspapers and magazines. Pulling the cart was a man. He wore a towel tied around his head and a dirty white T-shirt. Like a snail, he was inching ever so slowly up the slope.

"It's a scrap man," murmured Kazuo.

Scrap men bought people's old magazines and newspapers, empty bottles, iron scrap, and other unneeded items for low prices. On days when the weather was good, they walked through town pulling their carts, ringing a bell and calling, "Scrap man, will haul! Scrap man, will haul!"

Today, now that the weather had finally cleared, they were probably trying to catch up on work they had missed due to the rain.

Even Kazuo, at the top of the hill, could see that the cart, loaded with newspapers, was hindering the man's progress. For every step he took up the hill, the cart seemed to pull him a half step back down.

That's got to be hard, thought Kazuo. A moment later he realized there was someone else behind the cart.

That person was pressing both hands against the back of the cart and digging into the ground with both legs. His face was hidden behind the mountains of old newspapers. But with every step he took, his head—wrapped, like the scrap man's, in a towel made into a headband—bobbed up and down like a buoy.

After the two people had climbed slowly for a while, they stopped next to a telephone pole. They removed the towels from their heads and wiped the sweat from their faces.

Kazuo gasped in surprise. The scrap man's helper was his own classmate, Minoru. Kazuo instinctively ducked behind another telephone pole, hiding himself.

Minoru was a Korean who had grown up in Japan and lived in a neighborhood of shacks with tin roofs. It was the Korean quarter, located down the Haneto River, with its many small and medium-sized factories.

Minoru was completely hopeless at studying, but he was the biggest boy in fourth grade and so good at *sumo* that no one could defeat him. That had bothered Yukichi, the toughest kid in Kazuo's class. So one time, Yukichi had invited

Minoru over to the sandbox during lunch recess. Yukichi's older brother Masato, a very large fifth grader, had been waiting there.

"Hey, Minoru! I hear you said you never lose at *sumo*," Masato said, giving Minoru a hard stare.

"I didn't say I never lose. I said I was good at *sumo*, that's all." Minoru hunched his shoulders tensely on either side of his round, plump face.

> **Sumo**
>
> A Japanese sport where a wrestler (*rikishi*) tries to push another wrestler out of the ring (*dohyo*). *Sumo* has many ancient traditions, and some of its rituals (like throwing salt before a match) come from the Shinto religion. *Sumo* wrestlers may be huge, but they are more muscle than fat. They eat special foods to make them gain weight.

At the start of fourth grade, Kazuo's teacher, Mr. Honda, had said, "For the next year, you and I will be studying together. So I would like to get to know each of you well. To help me with that, please tell me something you are good at. Maybe you are good at drawing comics, or you're an expert on baseball players—it can be anything at all."

At that time, Minoru had answered that he was good at *sumo*. Now Yukichi and Masato were using Minoru's answer as an excuse to bully him.

"If you're so good at *sumo*," Masato went on, "why don't you and I have a match right here? I'll help you find out just how strong you are."

In a corner of the sandbox, Masato began to warm up like a professional *sumo* wrestler. He stood with his legs apart and bent his knees. Then he lifted one leg at a time out to the side, his hands on his thighs.

Kids began to gather around.

Yukichi smiled slyly, putting an arm around Minoru's

shoulders as if they were the best of pals. "How about it, Minoru? If you're so good at *sumo*, have a go with my brother."

Minoru twisted his lip and answered in a shaky voice. "Well, okay, but just once."

"Face your opponent!" At the command of Yukichi, who had assumed the role of referee, the two boys crouched in starting positions and touched the ground with their fingertips. Masato instantly leaped up and charged into Minoru. He grabbed Minoru's belt with his right hand, trying to knock him over.

"Uh oh, Minoru's going down!" everyone thought.

But a second later, the boy who hit the sand was not Minoru. It was Masato.

Minoru had waited until Masato was off-balance from trying to push him over. Then he'd thrown down the older boy.

Masato got to his feet, his entire back covered in sand. "I wasn't ready. One more round."

Masato again prepared to fight. This time he charged at Minoru while pushing at him in various places with his hands. But without retreating even one step, Minoru took the pushes in stride and grabbed Masato's body. As before, Masato ended up on his back in the center of the sandbox.

Furious to have lost twice in a row to a younger kid, Masato's face turned bright red. "One more round," he shouted, charging at Minoru. But the result was the same. In an instant, Masato went sprawling in the sand.

Everyone in Kazuo's class, except Yukichi and a few of

his friends, applauded for Minoru, who had defeated a fifth-grader three times. But being beaten so easily by a fourth-grader was more than the giant Masato could take.

Standing up slowly, Masato spit in the sand. "Stupid Korean! He stinks so much of garlic, you can't even wrestle him."

Minoru's round face, which always smiled good-naturedly and never showed anger, suddenly turned fierce. Then as Minoru clenched his jaw and glared at Masato, his face slowly crumpled. Standing there in the middle of the sandbox, he hid his face in the crook of his right arm.

He's crying, Kazuo realized.

Masato started mocking him again. "Korean pig. Korean pig!"

"Shut your trap, you jerk! What did Koreans ever do to you?"

A girl suddenly came flying out of the group gathered around the sandbox and went toward Masato. It was Hanae Yanagi, a realtor's daughter, and one of the top students in Kazuo's class.

But before she could reach the fifth-grader, a furious voice boomed across the playground.

"What are you doing over there?"

Everybody turned toward the voice. Mr. Honda was sprinting toward them with his hair flying up.

Kazuo could not remember Mr. Honda ever looking angry before. But at that moment, his face looked as scary as a demon's. He ran up at full speed and planted himself before Masato.

"What did you just say to Minoru Kaneda?"

"I called him a Korean pig," Masato answered without a sign of remorse. "He's a Korean, so I called him one. I didn't do anything wrong."

The next moment, an unbelievable scene unfolded before Kazuo's eyes.

Mr. Honda's pale hand came down hard on Masato's cheek, as if in slow motion. Mild-mannered Mr. Honda had hit a student! Everyone fell silent in shock. Even Yukichi, the ringleader of the incident, and Minoru, who had been crying, grew quiet and stared in disbelief.

"You ought to be ashamed of yourself as a human being," Mr. Honda continued. "You're a fifth-grader, yet you lose at *sumo* and have to go picking on a fourth-grader? Do you find that enjoyable? And have you no idea how shameful it is to discriminate against another person?"

The teacher seized Masato by the arm and marched him off to the office. Kazuo and the rest of his classmates, including Yukichi, remained silent, as if they were the ones being punished. They stayed that way even after they had returned to their classroom. Saying nothing, they waited quietly in their seats.

Soon Mr. Honda came in. His face was pale as he looked around at all of the students in the class. "First of all, I need to apologize. Today during lunch recess, when a fifth-grade student insulted Kaneda-kun, I grew very angry and hit that student. Using violence against other people is unacceptable under any circumstances. I was wrong to do what I did, and I would like to apologize to you."

The teacher bowed low before the class.

"I would, however, like everyone to understand why I got upset," Mr. Honda said, then wrote some characters on the chalkboard.

"These characters are read *sabetsu*, which means discrimination. This is making fun of, or looking down on, people because of the color of their skin, their nationality, or the way they look. It is a shameful practice, the one thing people should avoid doing at all costs. The reason I got upset today was because the older student made fun of Kaneda-kun's Korean nationality. There are other students besides Kaneda-kun in this school who are nationals of North Korea or South Korea."

Mr. Honda is talking about Hanae, Kazuo realized. When Minoru began to cry, she alone had confronted Masato. Kazuo was impressed that she had tried to take him on, even though she was a girl.

"Now why are there residents of Japan who have North Korean and South Korean nationality? They are known as *zainichi*, or resident, Koreans."

Kazuo listened as Mr. Honda explained that before World War II, Korea had been colonized by the Japanese. The people in Korea were forbidden to use their native language or their real names and were put to work like servants. Later on, during the war, when the male adults of Japan were off fighting as soldiers and there was a shortage of workers in coal mines and factories, many people from Korea and China were forcibly brought to Japan and made to work like slaves, without even getting enough to eat.

"So the Koreans living in Japan had their homes and livelihoods taken from them," Mr. Honda explained.

Kazuo listened uneasily. He had heard from his parents that during the war there were air raids almost every day, that life had been hard because food was scarce, and so on. He had been told that many people died in the atomic bombings of Hiroshima and Nagasaki and in the firebombings of Tokyo. He knew that war was very bad, bringing misery to many people.

But Mr. Honda had just said that the Japanese had ruled over Minoru and Hanae's parents, and grandparents, and their friends, and treated them like slaves. Everything the teacher had talked about, all those terrible things, had been done by people connected with Kazuo.

That day his discomfort made him decide one thing: from then on he would be kinder to Minoru and Hanae.

Now, as he stood on the hill behind the telephone pole, listening to the labored breathing of Minoru and his father, Kazuo wondered why he had jumped out of sight so quickly. He thought it was because Minoru might feel embarrassed to be seen pushing his scrap man father's cart. If it were Kazuo, he would feel shame, as if a dark secret had been revealed.

But Kazuo also wondered if his act might be called discrimination. Maybe Kazuo was looking down on the work that Minoru's father did, judging it as dirty and shameful. Kazuo felt a heavy lump deep down in his chest. Minoru and his father began to move the cart forward again. Soon Kazuo could hear Minoru's father shouting, "Scrap man, will haul!"

Kazuo knew he could still call out, "Minoru, how's it going?" And sturdy Minoru would probably just crinkle his round face into a smile and wave back.

But that is not what Kazuo did.

The sounds of the bell on the cart's handle and of Minoru's father calling out, "Scrap man! Will haul!" gradually moved away through the quiet town as sunlight flooded its streets.

Kazuo, still hidden in the shadow of the telephone pole, stood as if frozen, listening intently to those two sounds.

NISHINO-KUN'S HOUSE OF BOOKS

The other friend that Kazuo made in November was Akira Nishino. Nobuo and Minoru usually called him just Akira or by the nickname Nishiyan. But Kazuo eventually started to call him Nishino-**kun** out of respect.

Akira's father was a university professor, and his mother was an elementary school teacher. Not one other student in Kazuo's grade had a parent who was a teacher, and only a few students had a parent with a university degree. Most parents, like Kazuo's father, had gone straight to work after finishing their compulsory education.

Akira was polite to everyone, as well as kind. But when it came to his grades in school, he definitely did not fit Kazuo's expectations of a child of two teachers.

That was because Akira spent a lot of time absentmind-

-kun A suffix often used when speaking to boys in a respectful way. (It is never used with girls.) Kazuo calls Akira "Nishino-kun," using his friend's last name with the suffix, to express his respect for his friend's intelligence.

edly staring out the window. When he wasn't staring out the window, he seemed to be thinking about something completely different from what was being written on the chalkboard or explained by the teacher. When Mr. Honda pointed at him to answer a question, he would often give an answer that made no sense, making the kind teacher smile wryly. Akira seemed to have an especially hard time with math. He still made mistakes, even though he was in fourth grade now.

Still, Akira appeared to be acting a little more lively in school these days. Last year, with Mr. Tanaka, who was strict and lost his temper at the drop of a hat, Akira had gotten a scolding nearly every day. When he gave a wrong answer or made a mistake at math, Mr. Tanaka would say, "If you can't even handle this problem, don't you think your parents will be disappointed in you?"

And Akira would press his lips together and nod, his face the saddest in the entire world.

But one day in April, Kazuo had changed his opinion of his classmate.

During science, Mr. Honda had been talking about pistils and stamens in flowers, explaining that the reason flowers bloom on plants and trees is to produce seeds and fruit. Then he asked a question of Akira, calling him by his family name.

"Nishino-kun, why is it that flowers bloom on plants and trees?"

Akira, who had been staring out the window, turned red in the face. He remained silent, crossing his long, thin arms awkwardly in front of his body.

"You must not have heard my question," Mr. Honda said gently. "Very well, I will ask you again. Why is it that flowers bloom on plants and trees?"

Akira stared silently at the ceiling.

"How about it, did you think of something?" Mr. Honda prodded him.

"Perhaps . . ." he said in a small voice.

"Perhaps what?"

"Perhaps flowers bloom to get attention from people and insects and animals," Akira finally said.

Half of the students tittered. His answer was just too strange—as if plants and trees would flower for the same reason people get dressed up, to get attention.

"Everyone, please be quiet." The teacher silenced the laughter. "So, Nishino-kun, why do you think that is?"

Akira still spoke softly. "When flowers are in bloom, people and insects and animals are attracted to their colors and smells and go over to them. That probably makes it easier for the pollen to scatter, and easier to produce seeds and fruit."

Mr. Honda nodded vigorously several times, grinning broadly. And this time nobody laughed.

"Nishino-kun's response was an extremely good one," Mr. Honda said. Then he motioned for Akira to sit down. "Nishino-kun focused on the beauty and scent of flowers, and considered them within all of nature. It is exactly

Nihonjin

The Japanese word for "Japan" is 日本 *nihon*, written with the characters 日 *ni* for "sun" and 本 *hon* for "root." This is why Japan is sometimes called the Land of the Rising Sun. The character 人 *jin* means "person." So a Japanese person is a 日本人, or *nihonjin*.

as Nishino-kun has explained: flowers' beauty brings insects and animals closer, and makes the pollen on the stamens easier to scatter. This way the plants do not have to rely only on the wind to get the pollen to the pistils."

Listening to Mr. Honda, Kazuo began wondering about Akira, who had always seemed so absent-minded and slow to find the right answer. Maybe he was more interesting than Kazuo had realized. Maybe he had even more mysterious ideas inside his head. After this, Kazuo himself began to add the suffix "-kun" to Akira's family name as a sign of respect.

After Nishino-kun and Minoru ended up in the same group as Kazuo, the three of them often walked home together. Nobuo, and sometimes Yasuo, joined them, making them a group of five—the J-Boys. The boys said if they ever had a rock band, that was what they'd call themselves. In their own language they were *nihonjin*, but to Americans, they were "Japanese boys." That's what Nishino-kun had said, anyway, and the name just stuck.

On the days when the weather was fine, they always went to the empty lot. Nobuo and Kazuo had not yet given up on their Bob Hayes program. As soon as they got to the lot, they began talking back and forth about Bob Hayes.

Then they practiced starting low to the ground and charging into a sprint as they took off running.

Nishino-kun and Minoru sat on the wilted grass and watched them. Neither had ever heard of the great sprinter Bob Hayes from the Tokyo Olympics. Plus, Nishino-kun had ab-solutely no interest in sports, while Minoru knew the names of *sumo* wrestlers but nothing about the other sports.

> **Yokozuna**
>
> Grand master or grand champion, the highest rank in professional *sumo* wrestling. Once a wrestler reaches this rank he is expected to win most of his tournaments. There can be more than one *yokozuna* at a time.

Today, after Kazuo and Nobuo grew tired of their efforts, the four friends sat talking.

"What do you want to be in the future?" Nobuo asked suddenly. He was sprawled on the ground, his chin resting in his hand, which was propped up by one elbow.

"A *sumo* wrestler, of course." Minoru jumped up and got into the squat that wrestlers assume before a match, spreading his arms out wide. "I'm going to reach the **yokozuna** rank, live in a huge house, and eat good food every day until I'm bursting."

Nobuo grinned. "You're an eater, aren't you, Minoru!"

Minoru laughed self-consciously.

"I'm going to be a runner," Nobuo said, brimming with confidence. "I'm going to compete at the Olympics and win the gold medal. I'll run the hundred meters in one burst, just like Bob Hayes. But my time is going to be nine seconds flat, a new world record. How about that—impressive, huh?"

Watching Nobuo as he flared his nostrils and spoke

with gusto, Kazuo felt that one day his friend just might make his dream come true. Nobuo had been growing a lot recently and was now quite tall.

"And what do you want to be, Nishiyan?" Minoru asked. Nishino-kun had been listening to the other two with a quiet smile.

"I bet you'll be a college professor like your father," Nobuo interrupted before Nishino-kun could answer. "With all those books, it would be a waste if you didn't become one!"

Kazuo suddenly pictured the inside of Nishino-kun's house behind the shopping area. Two weeks ago, they had all gone there to play, taking Yasuo with them. Because Nishino-kun's parents were both educators, Kazuo had expected to see a white house with a triangular roof, like the houses in American TV shows. He'd imagined carpets on

Boys playing near a huge tree in a city park.

the floor, and chairs and tables, and the family drinking black tea or coffee.

But when Nishino-kun said, "This is it," and pointed to his house, Kazuo saw instead an aging wooden structure that looked exactly like every other house in West Ito. The exterior walls were covered in cedar boards that had weathered to a dark brown. The roof was a traditional black tile roof, and the front door was no different from the door to Kazuo's company housing unit: a sliding door with frosted glass windows. It was an extremely ordinary house.

Following Nishino-kun, the boys passed the Nishino Residence nameplate on the front gatepost and headed to the door. To the right of the path was a small garden.

"Hey, Nishino-kun, you could have a dog here!" Yasuo told him when he spotted the garden.

"Yasuo, is that the only thing you ever think about?" Kazuo said, and everybody laughed at his exasperated tone.

"Actually, I wish I could have a dog," Nishino-kun said.

"You should get one!" Yasuo agreed, excited.

But Nishino-kun smiled sadly. "My father won't let me. He says that having a dog would ruin the garden."

None of the boys knew why having a dog would ruin the garden. But if Nishino-kun's university-professor father said it would, they had to believe it.

Nishino-kun used a key to open the old door to the entryway. It slid to the side with a clatter, like a cart traveling through gravel. But when the four boys saw what appeared beyond it, their mouths dropped open.

Nishino-kun's house was crammed with books.

Entryway

In a house like Nishino-kun's, the front door is a sliding panel that opens onto an entryway (*genkan*) where visitors call to announce themselves or take off their shoes before entering the home (you never wear shoes inside a Japanese house or apartment). Often the rooms are separated by sliding panels (*fusuma*) that are a lot like movable walls, to be closed for privacy or opened for ventilation.

The **entryway** was typically a place where people sat or bent down to put their shoes on or take them off. At Nishino-kun's house, however, the books took up so much space that there was nowhere to sit down. Tall stacks of books were everywhere, lining both sides of the hallway leading into the interior of the house.

"Go on in." At Nishino-kun's urging, the boys ventured further inside, where the air smelled musty, like old paper. Yasuo clung to the bottom of Kazuo's sweater, looking as frightened as if he had lost his way in a haunted mansion.

"These sure are huge piles of books," Kazuo said to Nishino-kun. He tried to sound nonchalant as he gaped at all of the stacks, which seemed to have them surrounded. "Are they all your father's?"

"Yeah, they're his," Nishino-kun answered.

Kazuo noticed that more than half of the books were in foreign languages.

"Why don't we have some juice or something?" Nishino-kun suggested. He led them into the living room and brought some juice powder, cups, and a kettle of water from the kitchen. Kazuo and the others continued to look about uneasily, not touching the juice that Nishino-kun prepared in front of them.

Nobuo's eyes were fixed on some sliding doors at the

back of the room. A pine tree was painted on them. "Is there a room on the other side of those doors, too?"

"Yeah, that's my dad's study. Would you like to see it?" Nishino-kun stood up and opened the doors.

Kazuo saw yet another room overflowing with books. It did not look like it was even used by humans. With just a tiny bit of afternoon sunlight streaming in through an opening in the curtains, it looked more like something from a science-fiction movie.

All the walls of the six-mat room had large bookcases placed against them. Books that did not fit into the bookcases were piled into towering stacks on the floor. Kazuo thought they looked like skyscrapers built by aliens. He could even picture a creature with an oversized head and detached eyeballs sitting at the desk in the middle of the room and ruling over the alien city.

And so, two weeks later, as the boys sat in the empty lot talking about their futures, Nobuo was obviously remembering all the books in Nishino-kun's house, too. But when he asked Nishino-kun if he were going to be a college professor, Nishino-kun shook his head. "That would be impossible. I'm not very smart, you know." He wrapped his long, skinny arms around his legs and looked away.

"You're smart," Kazuo spoke up.

"Yeah," Nobuo chimed in. "If you don't want to be a college professor, then what do you want to do?"

Nishino-kun stayed silent. He just kept staring off at the wilted, brown grass.

Kazuo exchanged glances with the others. He couldn't help feeling annoyed with Nishino-kun. His family was well off, at least compared to the rest of them. Both of his parents were teachers, and he had a ton of books in his household. He ought to be able to do anything he wanted when he got older.

"Akira!" someone said sharply.

Kazuo turned around. A thin man wearing a gray suit and glasses was coming toward them.

"Otohsan!" Nishino-kun scrambled to his feet.

Nishino-kun's father approached the boys with deliberate strides. "These must be your friends." He held a bulging briefcase, and his forehead was furrowed as he glanced at Kazuo and the others.

"Yes," Nishino-kun answered in a small voice.

"Is your homework done yet?"

"No, not yet." Nishino-kun hung his head.

"Well then, instead of loitering in a place like this, I want you to go straight home and study. Do I make myself clear?" Nishino-kun's father spoke in a low, stern voice.

Nishino-kun nodded, then picked up his backpack.

"I'll see you tomorrow, everyone," he muttered. He hunched his shoulders as he followed his father out of the lot.

"He's heading home to that house of his," Minoru murmured.

Kazuo knew exactly what Minoru was saying. In that house of his, Nishino-kun probably had to study under the stern eye of his father. Kazuo himself studied while being nagged by his mother. But that was in the living room with the TV on, and plenty of ways to escape her instructions. Nishino-kun's house, which seemed to exist for the sole purpose of storing books, probably didn't have any escape routes.

A chilly wind had begun to blow though the empty lot. Without anybody saying much of anything, Kazuo, Nobuo, and Minoru got up and put on their backpacks.

"Well, see you," Minoru said.

"Yeah, see you tomorrow," Nobuo answered.

"Bye." Kazuo waved and started for home. As he walked, he thought again about Nishino-kun and how he'd refused to say anything about his future plans. Why had he acted so stubborn? Kazuo wondered. Then he remembered how Nishino-kun acted in class, all dreamy with his unusual way of thinking that Mr. Honda seemed to admire. Nishino-kun was different, that was for sure. But maybe like the other boys, he did dream about his future. It was just that he had trouble expressing that dream in words because of the mountains of books in his house, or because of that low, stern voice that told him to "go straight home and study."

Kazuo smiled when he remembered what he himself had said about what he wanted to be when he grew up. He hadn't answered with his father's words: "Kazuo will enter a national university, get a Ph.D., and work at a top company!" Instead he'd said the first thing that had popped into his head.

"I think I'll be the captain of a ship that goes to foreign countries."

"That's cool," Minoru had said. The others had grinned and nodded.

Kazuo was nearly home. The sun had set and the sky was nearly black now.

Being the captain of a ship does sound cool, Kazuo thought. He wondered if he'd really do it. He wondered what the future held for any of the J-Boys.

Boys playing in an empty lot.

What Wimpy Ate

By now Kazuo knew a lot about American foods from watching American TV shows. From school lunch, he'd learned to twirl his spaghetti around inside his spoon. When he ate spinach, he imagined getting strong like **Popeye**. And when he had cheese, he felt a bit like the mouse in **Tom and Jerry** cartoons. The *miruku* he had to drink was as disgusting as ever, of course.

But there was one food that Kazuo could not figure out. That was the food that had meat between two round pieces of bread. It was eaten by Wimpy, a fat man who often appeared on *Popeye the Sailor*.

"I'll gladly pay you Tuesday for a *hanbaagaa* today," Wimpy always said.

Why next Tuesday, Kazuo did not know, but a *hanbaagaa* had to be delicious if it was worth borrowing money for.

"I bet it's some kind of croquette roll," Nobuo had told Kazuo.

Popeye

An American comic strip and cartoon hero who speaks with a raspy voice and gains super-strength from popping open and eating whole cans of spinach. *Popeye the Sailor*, with the Japanese title *Popai*, was shown in Japan from 1959 to 1965.

Tom and Jerry

Cat and mouse cartoon characters famous for their wild chases and frantic fights. The first *Tom and Jerry* cartoon appeared around 1940. In Japan, *Tom and Jerry* was broadcast from 1964 to 1966.

Croquette

Korokke in Japanese. A deep-fried breaded patty of minced meat or fish mixed with potato, eggs, and breadcrumbs. *Korokke* are filling, cheap, and convenient, one of the original "fast foods" in Japan.

A **croquette** roll, which consisted of a crispy croquette sandwiched between two halves of a bread roll, was certainly delicious. But a croquette roll was hardly the sort of food you'd borrow money for.

So Kazuo wasn't so sure about Nobuo's theory.

Kazuo tried asking his friend Nishino-kun, but he had no idea either. "I'll ask my father sometime."

Kazuo didn't think that Nishino-kun's stern father would know about Wimpy's *hanbaagaa*. But Nishino-kun's father was a college professor, after all, so Kazuo allowed himself a faint hope.

And one morning, two days later, Nishino-kun excitedly informed the other boys that he had found out what a *hanbaagaa* was.

"My father says it's really called a *hanburugu* steak," Nishino-kun said, taking a slip of paper from his backpack.

"*Hanbaagaa*. Alternative name for *hanburugu* steak. A grilled patty of ground beef mixed with flour, onion, and similar ingredients."

Kazuo felt confused about the word "steak." He knew what "beefsteak" was: a thick slab of grilled beef that was served on a plate. But that was completely different from the food Wimpy picked up with his hands to eat.

"It sounds like a breaded ground pork patty," Nobuo said.

Kazuo shook his head. "No, it's different from a pork patty." He was certain about that much.

Meanwhile, the weather had turned cold. At Kazuo's house, the heated table, or **kotatsu**, appeared in the living room in December after being shut away from spring through autumn. There was nothing quite like sitting at the *kotatsu*, a low table with an electric heater attached to its underside. Coming in from the cold outdoors and putting your legs and arms underneath the blanket that covered the table was like dipping yourself into rays of warm sunshine. Kazuo and Yasuo spent so much time sitting there, with their limbs tucked underneath and their chins resting on the tabletop, that their mother would say, "You're going to sprout roots and be stuck there, even when spring comes."

But the boys continued to linger at the *kotatsu*, even after their parents left for work in the mornings. They would jump out and run off to school only when they were almost late.

Part of the reason for this was that if they arrived too

Obaachan

Grandma. Similar to other name forms, this is a less formal form of *Obaasan*, or Grandmother.

Nagauta

A form of traditional Japanese vocal music. It was originally used in Kabuki (historical costume drama) to comment on the action from the side of the stage. The *nagauta* singer often plays a *shamisen*, a three-stringed instrument that sounds a bit like a banjo.

early, their classrooms would be freezing cold.

Every classroom at the school had a coal-burning stove. But the teacher didn't put the coal in and light the stove until right before first period. Plus, the boys in Kazuo's class liked daring each other to see who could wear shorts to school the longest. As long as their game continued, the cold of the winter mornings would seem even worse.

On the first Saturday afternoon of December, Kazuo and Yasuo arrived home from school to find a pair of women's wooden sandals in the entryway.

Grandmother! Kazuo thought, hearing an older woman's lively voice on the other side of the door to the living room.

"I think **Obaachan**'s here!" Yasuo cried.

Grandmother was taking lessons twice a month in *nagauta*, traditional folk singing. She often stopped by Kazuo's house when her lessons fell on a Saturday.

This grandmother was their mother's mother, Tatsue, and Kazuo was happy that she had come. But he was too old now to show excitement like Yasuo. He intentionally removed his shoes slowly before stepping into the living room.

"Hello there, Kazuo. I think you've gotten taller again!" Grandmother, who was wearing a light brown *kimono* with a deep green **haori** jacket, turned to look at him from the *kotatsu*.

> **Haori**
>
> A lightweight silk jacket worn over a *kimono* to protect it and keep it clean and dry. You can read more about *kimono* on page 128.
>
> **Obi**
>
> A sash for a *kimono*. *Obi* for women come in many different widths, colors, and patterns and can be over 12 feet long. Wide *obi* are for formal occasions, and colorful *obi* are for younger, unmarried women. An *obi* requires a lot of practice to put on and tie correctly (often an assistant is needed!).

"Maybe I've gotten taller. I'm not sure." Kazuo sat down next to his grandmother. He smelled something that reminded him of herbal mouth-freshening drops. He thought the scent was from a small sachet in Grandmother's **obi**.

"Kazuo, did you greet Obaachan properly?" Mother asked, bringing a plate of tangerines from the kitchen.

"You sure did, didn't you, Kazuo?" Grandmother said. She smiled as if they were sharing a joke.

Mother sat across from Kazuo and gave him a look. "Don't spoil him too much, Okaasan. He talks back and ignores me quite enough these days without your encouragement." Mother lightly slapped the top of Kazuo's hand as he reached for a tangerine.

"Wash your hands first. Then you can eat."

"My, my, you have a strict mother, don't you?" his grandmother said. He got up to wash his hands and then returned to the *kotatsu*.

"Here, Kazuo." Grandmother handed him a peeled tangerine.

"Koji-san is late today, isn't he?" Grandmother said, asking about Father.

Businesses closed for the week at noon on Saturdays, just like school. Father was usually home before one o'clock.

"They have extra work to finish before the end of the year. He won't be home till late afternoon," Mother said.

"Too bad," Grandmother said, sounding disappointed. "I was hoping to take everyone out for lunch."

"You mean it? All *right*!" Yasuo said.

"But we should wait until another time since your father isn't home. It's more fun when we can all go together."

Yasuo's shoulders instantly drooped.

Grandmother laughed and slapped his back.

With his chest hunched and the chin of his sulky face resting on the tabletop, Yasuo looked like a deflated rubber doll.

"Well, how about this. I'll take you and Kazuo on a date, just the three of us."

"A date?" Yasuo blinked in surprise.

"What, you don't like that idea?"

"It's not that I don't like it, but it sounds a little embarrassing."

"Well, all right then." Grandmother put her arm around Kazuo's shoulders. "Kazuo and I will just have to go all by ourselves."

"Hey, that's not fair!" Yasuo cried. "You have to take me with you, too!"

Grandmother laughed again. "All right then, let's get going while it's still warm out."

Before long the three of them were walking through the fancy **Ginza** district downtown, which was decked out in red, gold, white, and green to celebrate the Christmas season. There were Christmas trees covered in miniature lights everywhere, and the song "Jingle Bells" was playing down every street.

An upscale shopping district in downtown Tokyo. A trip to Ginza was a very special event (the area is several train stops north of where Kazuo lives). The Mitsukoshi Department Store was (and still is) a landmark building, filled with floors of expensive merchandise and lots of restaurants where shoppers can eat and relax.

Ginza

"Yasuo, hold tight to my *kimono* so we don't lose each other," Grandmother said as they continued on their way to the restaurant. She dropped a one-hundred-yen bill into a donation pot at the Sukiyabashi intersection, where a Salvation Army chorus was singing "Silent Night."

Soon, they reached the cafeteria on the eighth floor of the Mitsukoshi Department Store. The place was packed, with not one single seat available. There were already two families waiting in line ahead of them, sitting on chairs outside the cafeteria.

A middle-aged man in a bow tie told them politely that it would be a thirty-minute wait.

"We're not in a hurry, so that will be fine," Grandmother replied. She turned to Kazuo and Yasuo, who were already sitting in the chairs.

"I've just remembered a little errand I have to run. You

boys sit here like grown-ups for a few minutes and wait for me to come back."

Then she hurried off.

"Hey, do you think Obaachan went to telephone our grandpa?" Yasuo whispered. Kazuo was looking at the **waxlike models** of the food served in the cafeteria, which were displayed in a glass case.

"Probably," Kazuo said, then added sharply, "but remember, Yasuo, you absolutely cannot tell Okaasan that we saw Ojiichan."

Kazuo had been four years old when he first met his grandfather. Until that point, he'd been told that he didn't have one.

He had learned from picture books that there were people called grandfathers, and that they were older men, with white hair and slightly bent backs, who would take their grandchildren for walks. When he asked his parents why he didn't have a grandfather, his mother had always answered, "Your father's father passed away before you were born, and my father has gone very far away, so there is no grandfather in our family."

"Where is far away?" Kazuo had asked more than once.

And his mother replied stubbornly, "Far away means very, very far away."

When Kazuo asked his grandmother about it, she didn't answer either. Instead, her mouth just formed a perplexed frown.

But one day in the spring of the year he turned four, something happened. In the cafeteria on the eighth floor of the Mitsukoshi Department Store—the same place they were today—Grandmother had said, "This is your Ojiichan, Soichiro Kuramoto."

Kazuo, suddenly confronted by his real grandfather, had burst out crying in confusion. And just like the grandfathers in the picture books, Grandfather had been very nice, ordering curry rice and ice cream, the things he liked. Kazuo had gradually stopped crying, reassured by the man's kindness.

Later, back at home, Kazuo had said to his mother, "I met Ojiichan today." The moment she heard those words, his mother had flown into a rage at Grandmother. Eventually Kazuo pieced together what had happened. Grandfather had opposed Mother's marriage to Father because Father had only gone to vocational school, not to university. Also, Mother, who had finished high school and was working for a trading company, had been promised to another family by her parents long before. Mother had hated the idea of an arranged marriage and had run away to marry Father.

After leaving, she had never attempted to see her own father again. Kazuo had once heard his mother say to his grandmother, "The war was over and we were living in a democracy, yet he saw nothing wrong with forcing me into a marriage? Until he apologizes, I have no desire to see him, even until death."

Sometimes their grandmother would shake her head

and say to Kazuo and Yasuo, "They're both so stubborn, I don't know what to do."

But Kazuo could not imagine Grandfather being angry with Mother. That was because, when he was with Kazuo and Yasuo, he was the nicest person in the world. Even when Yasuo pulled a silly prank, or Kazuo and Yasuo started to quarrel in the cafeteria, Grandfather didn't raise his voice. He only reminded them gently, with a smile, that they "mustn't do that."

And it was impossible for Kazuo to imagine Grandfather speaking ill of Father on the basis of his education. But Kazuo was beginning to understand why Father seemed to harp at them all the time to study so they'd get into a national university.

Now, while waiting for Grandmother to return, Kazuo stared at the food models inside the glass case at the restaurant. The brightly colored models of fried breaded shrimp, spaghetti, fried rice omelet, curry rice, and other dishes made the food look very fancy and delicious.

They're trying to make it look better than it actually is, to get people to order something, Kazuo thought. He started to look away. But then a white label at the far end caught his eye: *Hanburugu* Steak.

"*Hanburugu* steak. *Hanburugu* steak." There was no model behind the label, but Kazuo instantly knew what the food was: *hambaagaa*. "Alternative name for *hanburugu* steak. A grilled patty of ground beef mixed with flour, onion, and similar ingredients."

Kazuo could feel his heart thudding in his chest.

Finally he could taste the *hanbaagaa* that Wimpy was always eating!

Kazuo could barely stand still. Already he was thinking about how on Monday morning he would tell his friends about the delicious *hanbaagaa* he'd eaten.

"Oniichan, are you okay?" Yasuo asked, noticing Kazuo's sudden restlessness.

"Oh, it's nothing," Kazuo said, forcing himself to hide his smile.

Just as Kazuo and Yasuo had predicted, their grandmother soon returned with their grandfather. He was wearing a brown suit and an orange necktie.

"That's a pretty nice tie, Ojiichan," Yasuo said to Grandfather, whose eyes, framed by wrinkles, twinkled behind his glasses.

"You think so, Yasuo? Why, thank you. I got dressed up since I was coming to see you." When they were finally seated, Grandfather asked how school was going.

"So-so, I guess," Kazuo answered.

"So-so, I guess," mimicked Yasuo.

A waitress came over, carrying cups of water and menus. Even as he was opening the menu that had been handed to him, Kazuo was already searching for the words "*hanburugu* steak." Next to him Yasuo was running his mouth as always. "Hmm, maybe I'll have curry rice this time, or a sandwich. Or I could order ..."

Kazuo scanned the menu again. But he could not find *hanburugu* steak anywhere.

I wonder if I was seeing things, he thought.

Tempura
Breaded, deep-fried seafood or vegetables, introduced to Japan by the Portuguese in the 1600s. Onion rings at an American restaurant are similar to tempura, but a tempura chef will deep fry broccoli, carrots, sweet potatoes, shrimp, and other ingredients.

Finally, he spotted the words written by hand at the very end of the menu. The price was three hundred yen. Curry rice was one hundred and fifty yen, and the expensive **tempura** set and grilled eel on rice were each two hundred yen. If Mother were along, she would say, "Three hundred yen! Absolutely not! That's much too expensive for a child!"

"What would you like, Yasuo?" Grandmother asked when the waitress returned.

"Curry rice, please," Yasuo answered.

"And for you, Kazuo?"

Kazuo took a breath before turning to face his grandparents.

"Actually, there is a food that I would like to eat, but I wonder if it's all right to order it," he said hesitantly.

"What is it, my boy? Go ahead and say it, anything you want," Grandfather said.

"It's a little bit on the expensive side . . ."

"Children shouldn't worry about prices," Grandfather said. "You order what you like."

Nudged along by his grandfather's words, Kazuo looked up at the waitress.

"I would like the *hanburugu* steak, please," he said carefully.

"My, you went for something very modern," his grandfather told him, laughing. "I think I'll have the tempura set."

Kazuo's grandmother went last, ordering the *udon* with egg. Then the waitress took their menus and left.

It seemed like it took forever for her to return.

When she finally wove back through the tables, Kazuo could see a tray of food in her hand.

On that tray is *hanbaagaa*, he thought.

First she served the curry rice to Yasuo. Next was Grandmother's *udon* with egg, and then came Grandfather's tempura set. Finally, on a white plate came . . .

"Oh!" The moment he saw the dish placed before him, a sound escaped Kazuo's mouth.

"Did I make a mistake?" The waitress checked her order list. "You did order *hanburugu* steak, didn't you?"

"Kazuo, you ordered *hanburugu* steak, so this will be fine, won't it?" Grandmother looked perplexed at Kazuo's reaction.

"Yes, this will be just fine." Kazuo answered in very formal fashion, and forced a smile.

But the food on the plate in front of him was completely wrong. It was not at all like the *hanbaagaa* that Wimpy ate on *Popeye the Sailor*.

The plate in front of Kazuo held an oval-shaped patty with a fried egg on top of it, and some cabbage and white rice on the side. Kazuo understood now that this patty of ground beef was *hanburugu* steak. The *hanbaagaa* that Wimpy ate was something different—this kind of steak sandwiched between two round pieces of bread.

"Well, then, shall we?" Kazuo's grandfather said, picking up his chopsticks.

Kazuo reached for the bottle of Worcestershire sauce that was on the table. He put some of it on his steak, and then used a fork to cut it. The ground beef was a little hard, but the taste was not bad. In fact, it was far more delicious than the white stew and curry stew that he had had at school, and it might just be the most delicious food he had ever tasted.

At least that is what he told himself. Being able to eat delicious food is a kind of happiness, so he must be an extremely happy person right now, he thought—as long as he did not think about how his meal was not the same as what Wimpy ate.

On the way home, Grandfather and Grandmother rode the train with Kazuo and Yasuo to West Ito Station. Kazuo and Yasuo said good-bye to them and then walked alone through the shopping area, which was crowded with evening shoppers.

"Oniichan, your *hanburugu* steak was good, huh?" Yasuo said, looking up at Kazuo.

At the restaurant, Kazuo had divided his last bite of *hanburugu* steak and given half to Yasuo.

"Yeah, it wasn't bad."

"Next time I'm going to order *hanburugu* steak, too," Yasuo said. "But we'd better not tell Okaasan that we saw Ojiichan today."

Yasuo went on talking, but Kazuo was thinking about something else: how to explain today's events to his friends on Monday morning. Could he say that he had eaten a **hanbaagaa**? Maybe. According to Nishino-kun's father, a *hanburugu* steak and *hanbaagaa* were the same thing.

Kazuo suddenly spotted a girl in the crowd who was about the same age as Yasuo. She was walking alongside a man who was probably her father, holding his hand. She was chattering on and on while wearing a big smile. Her father smiled back.

Mother was a little girl like that once, Kazuo realized suddenly. And she had probably held hands with Grandfather and walked along smiling at him, too. So maybe someday they would make up because, after all, he was her father and she was his daughter.

But Kazuo did not know which thing would happen first. Would he eat a real hamburger, the kind that Wimpy liked? Or would Okaasan and Ojiichan finally begin talking to each other again?

Pet Phrases
(or Mother and the War)

Everybody has certain pet phrases. Kazuo had recently begun to notice this.

First, there was the phrase that all grown-ups used: "During the war . . ." referring to World War II, which had ended about twenty years ago. Whenever adults lectured kids about something, telling them to do their homework or clean their plates, they always said, "During the war we couldn't study, even if we wanted to." Or, "During the war we couldn't be choosy about our food because there was no food."

Kazuo had heard this phrase so many times that he had begun to ignore it.

Then there were his father's pet phrases: "I'm beat" and, when he had been drinking, "Son, you are going to study hard and get into a good school, you hear me?"

Father could be heard saying "I'm beat" at least three times a day: after work when he arrived home, after dinner when he settled down to watch TV in the living room, and after TV time, when the low table had been cleared away and he was crawling into his bedding. He was saying it more now that the end of the calendar year was approaching and things were busy at work.

Kazuo believed that Father actually was really tired. Every morning he left for work at seven thirty and didn't come home until after seven. But on holidays and Sundays, Kazuo wished his father wouldn't say "I'm beat" quite so often. Saying it when he was sprawled in front of the TV was, in Kazuo's opinion, a little bit embarrassing.

Then there were Kazuo's mother's pet phrases. Not a day went by when they didn't hear "Boys, during the war . . ." The next most frequent ones were "Clean your plate," "Be grateful for what you have," "Straighten up," and "Did you do your homework?" The difference between Mother and Father's pet phrases was that Mother's were always directed at Kazuo and Yasuo.

Why doesn't Okaasan have a pet phrase about herself, like Otohsan does? Kazuo often wondered.

Perhaps it was because he and Yasuo always quarreled and had to be told to do their homework, and wanted to do nothing but watch TV and read comics.

Still, Kazuo didn't think he and Yasuo were really all that bad. They set the table before meals and folded up their own bedding. Their grades, while far from highest in their classes, were not bad. So Kazuo often wished that his mother would sometimes direct her pet phrases at her own life.

Recently, Mother had developed a new pet phrase: "I am sick and tired of war." This phrase came out of her mouth

Vietnam War
Waged between the United States and North Vietnam in Southeast Asia in the 1960s. One of the weapons used by the U.S. was a chemical for creating destructive fires in forests, fields, and villages. Many people died on both sides.

every time she saw images of the **Vietnam War**, which were beginning to appear constantly on the TV news.

One day in the middle of December, when Father was working late and Mother, Kazuo, and Yasuo had finished dinner, Mother said the phrase again.

They had been watching the seven o'clock news. The TV screen showed American warplanes heading into the jungles of North Vietnam and dropping bombs. Kazuo thought the scenes looked like images from a movie—unreal and even a little bit thrilling.

But that was not what Mother saw. "Why do people have to go and do that?" she said in a choked voice.

Startled, Kazuo and Yasuo looked at her. As she watched the TV, tears flowed from her eyes. The two boys, who had never seen their mother act like this, kept silent, stealing glances at her face from time to time.

After a while, the scene on the news changed to a bustling Tokyo street. Mother wiped her tears and shifted her gaze back to Kazuo and Yasuo.

"Do you want to hear what I have to say?" she asked quietly.

The two boys nodded, still keeping silent. What on earth was she about to tell them? Kazuo wondered. He shifted uneasily on the floor.

What she told them was a story they had never heard before. "During the war I lived apart from my family for two years, when I was in the fifth and sixth grade, due to the evacuation of school-children from Tokyo. But after sixth grade, when I'd graduated from grade school, I had to come back to Tokyo. I arrived in January of 1945.

"At that time, it was clear that Japan was losing the war. After all, American airplanes were dropping bombs on the streets of Tokyo almost every day. One of the most devastating attacks was the bombing of Shitama-chi, the old downtown.

"On March 9, the American military used incendiary bombs, or **firebombs**, for the first time. An incendiary bomb is filled with gasoline instead of gunpowder. The incendiary bombs turned all of the old downtown into a sea of fire. Many houses burned, and close to a hundred thousand people lost their lives. Mr. and Mrs. Yoshino, the owners of the tofu store, lost their son that night.

Firebombs

Bombs used in a series of raids conducted in 1945 by the United States Army Air Forces on Tokyo, Nagoya, Osaka, Kobe, and other Japanese cities. Japanese homes were primarily made of wood and paper, so the fires that resulted were intense. Hundreds of thousands of civilians died, and parts of the cities became like an inferno, with buildings bursting spontaneously into flame and people dying from the searing heat and lack of oxygen. For Kazuo's mother, the firebombings were still fresh and horrifying memories some twenty years after they happened.

"When that happened, I was living in Shibuya in west Tokyo. I watched with my own eyes as a firestorm filled the sky to the east, and the night turned a deep red, as bright as day. A lot of people jumped into the Sumida River to try and escape the heat. But the fire had eaten up every inch of the ground, and easily crossed the water, so everybody who jumped into the river was burned to death.

"When I heard that, I grew so stiff with fear that I couldn't move. I couldn't help wondering if the same kind of disaster would happen to me. An odd superstition was beginning to make the rounds then: if you only ate shallots for dinner, you would be able to outrun the fires from incendiary bombs. My mother—your grandmother—began to serve meals made only of shallot and sweet potato gruel."

"Oh . . ." Yasuo said sympathetically, as if he couldn't imagine such a dish as his only meal. Kazuo shot him a glance.

"But the bombs weren't just falling on Tokyo. They were falling on Osaka, Nagoya, Fukuoka—all around the country. And just as I had feared, the American military soon carried out an attack on western Tokyo, including Shibuya.

"The air raid started on May 24, after midnight. Your grandmother and I were the only ones home. When we heard the warning siren, we jumped out of our blankets. Outside the house, we could hear the B-29s as they flew in low. When they dropped their firebombs in the distance, it sounded just like rain falling in big drops on rooftops. The two of us grabbed bags packed with a change of clothes and our bank records, and ran out of the house.

"The sky to the south was deep red. We could tell that the firebombs were coming closer. I said to your grandmother, 'Okaasan, come on, let's go to the woods behind the Hachiman Shrine.' Soon we met up with a whole crowd of people also headed toward the shrine. Your grandma and I joined the crowd, gripping hands so we wouldn't get separated. But soon, the pitter-patter rain sounds shifted to loud whistling sounds, like flutes.

"And then, right before my eyes, columns of fire came crashing down. We all fell to the ground. The earth shook violently, then flames shot up everywhere, and in an instant the whole area was on fire.

"'If we stay here we'll burn to death!' somebody yelled. Everyone scrambled to their feet and began to run, desperately trying to get away. We moved with the crowd, rushing toward the woods behind the shrine.

"'You can't go that way!' someone else yelled. 'It's too dangerous! Go back!'

"Your grandmother and I both heard that voice, and we stopped in our tracks. But a lot of people around us couldn't hear it and kept running for the shrine. As the two of us stood frozen, wondering what to do, we heard the whistling sound like a flute, and then a bomb dropped right there in front of us. We were so scared, our bodies trembled like leaves as we fell to the ground. When we somehow managed to lift our heads, we saw just ahead of us a woman with a baby on her back. She'd been running for safety like us. Now she lay on the ground, her whole body on fire. The flames were so bad, we couldn't get close enough to help. The smell of gasoline filled the air, along with another horrible smell—the smell of human flesh burning. We could tell that the flames around us were getting higher and higher and closer and closer.

"'We'll die if we stay here!' I told your grandmother.

"Somehow the two of us got back on our feet, still shaking. Clutching each other's hand, we began to walk in the direction of smaller flames. The heat of the fire was so intense, it singed our eyebrows. We had no idea how long we walked. But eventually we realized we were standing in front of our own house.

"The fire was everywhere by now. 'If we're going to die,' your grandmother said, 'then we should die together in our own house.'

"The two of us went back inside. We huddled together on the bedding, trembling. By that point we could no longer hear the firebombs. Instead, we heard the roaring of the fire. I said a prayer: 'If we're going to die, let us die without suffering. And if we are born again, let us be born into a peaceful world with no war.'

"Finally, it began to grow light outside. Night was ending and morning had come.

"*We're still alive.* With this thought in our minds, we cautiously opened the front door.

"Outside, everything was gone. All the houses and buildings between our house and Shibuya Station had burned—not a single one was left standing. The area all around was flat and charred black as far as we could see. Off in the distance was Shinjuku Station, a building two stations away that we shouldn't have been able to see at all. Your grandmother and I took one look and began to weep. Here and there you could still see black smoke rising where fires were smoldering. The stench was so awful we could barely breathe. I was terrified I'd never see my relatives and friends again. And I remember looking at the field of ashes and thinking, 'So this is what death is.'"

Mother paused to take a breath. "Almost twenty years have gone by since the war ended, but the sights from that day will always haunt me.

"It turned out that everyone who fled to the Hachiman Shrine was burned to death because the fire spread to the trees in the woods. If we hadn't heard that voice warning us to go back, your mother and grandmother would no longer be in this world."

Both Kazuo and Yasuo listened to their mother with serious expressions. By now, she had told them many times about how there wasn't enough food during and after the war, and about how as a child she had studied with miniature light bulbs during blackouts, and about how lots of people had died during air raids. But this was a new story. Maybe she had decided to tell them about this because of the bombs flashing on their TV screen every night like a movie.

Kazuo had looked at a map, and America and Vietnam were far apart, on opposite sides of the Pacific Ocean. So why did America have to send so many troops and drop so many bombs in Vietnam? He had no idea. He also had no idea why his favorite American TV programs, like *Leave It to Beaver*, never showed the war. Instead, all they showed was the family's house with the big refrigerator, and Beaver's older brother coming home from school and making himself a sandwich, and the whole family wearing nice clothes. There was never an air raid siren going off, or people running frantically to get away from enemy planes dropping bombs.

All of this struck Kazuo as strange, but it didn't make him hate America. Instead, the America that appeared on the TV screen continued to look cheerful and wonderful to him.

After Kazuo's mother told the story, he expected things to change for some reason. He thought that maybe she would stop nagging them about their homework or about eating all the food on their plates. But even though she began to use the new pet phrase "I'm sick and tired of war" more often, her old pet phrases for Kazuo and his brother did not let up even a little.

When the two of them were engrossed in TV or comics, she asked, "Did you do your homework?" When they didn't eat their vegetables, she said, "Clean your plate." And if they complained that they would like to taste a steak like the ones Beaver and his family had for dinner, she would snap back at them with one of her favorite pet phrases, "Be grateful for what you have."

So Kazuo and Yasuo had to keep on doing their homework and cleaning their plates of onions and carrots and boiled fish, all the while remembering to be grateful for what they had.

Christmas and Report Cards

Kazuo did not like to study. He did his homework because he had to; not once had he ever wished to study more on his own. If he had extra time, he would much rather use it to play with his friends in the empty lot, or read comics, or watch TV.

Of course, he had privately vowed to study harder when the owner of Yoshino's Tofu Shop died, but that had not led to anything lasting. Kazuo knew that he wasn't putting as much effort into his schoolwork as he could, so when the end of fall term and report card day came on December 25, Christmas Day, he felt doomed from the moment he woke up.

Kazuo knew from TV and magazines that Christmas was the day Jesus Christ was born. He knew that in America and Europe, people put up Christmas trees and ate whole roasted turkey, and that children opened presents in front of glowing fireplaces.

Kazuo knew this, but he had never experienced it. At

his house, they never put up a Christmas tree, or ate a whole roasted turkey.

"Japanese people have New Year's. Surely that's enough." This was Kazuo's mother's explanation for why they didn't celebrate Christmas. Of course, when she put it that way, Kazuo had to agree. He had never been to church, or offered thanks to Jesus Christ before a meal, like the families did at supper on TV Westerns. He did not think of Jesus Christ's birthday as a reason to feel particularly grateful.

Then again, Christmas seemed much more stylish than New Year's, and Kazuo couldn't help finding everything about it more impressive. Compared with New Year's pine decorations, Christmas trees were far more splendid and eye-catching. And next to rice-dumpling soup and the salty-sweet dishes that were stored in lacquer boxes for New Year's, a whole turkey or chicken roasted to a tantalizing light brown seemed much more appetizing.

Of course, nobody in Kazuo's neighborhood actually put up a Christmas tree and celebrated the holiday like people did on American TV shows. The stores in the shopping area played Christmas songs nonstop, but the only ones with Christmas trees were the cake shop, Mimasu Sweets, and the toy shop, Tanaka. Then there was Takahashi Meats, owned by Nobuo's family, which sold specially roasted chicken thighs on Christmas Day only.

So Kazuo's Christmas celebration consisted almost entirely of eating a slice of **Christmas cake**, purchased by one of his parents, after dinner on December 25. And most of the pleasure from that had already been ruined by the handing out of report cards earlier in the day.

At school this year on Christmas Day, even the boys who usually loitered at the back of the classroom until the teacher came, talking loudly or pretending to be pro wrestlers, were waiting quietly in their seats. None of them could stop thinking about the report cards that were about to be handed out.

> A sponge cake topped with whipped cream and strawberries and sometimes chocolates or other fruit. It is usually eaten on Christmas Eve. Only a very small percentage of Japanese are Christian, but Japanese people enjoy many Christmas customs.
>
> **Christmas cake**

Eventually, Mr. Honda came into the classroom carrying the documents under his arm. Seeing everyone's tense faces, his eyes sparkled behind his glasses.

"When I was about your age, I hated report card day, too. Please remember, boys and girls, that low grades are an opportunity to work harder next term. And even if your grades have improved, there is still room to go up."

Mr. Honda handed the report cards to the students as they filed one-by-one to the front of the classroom. Like everyone, Kazuo took his report card from Mr. Honda and then went to his seat and opened it just a crack. He had gotten fives again in math, science, and physical education. (Five was the top grade on a scale of one to five.) He'd gotten fours in Japanese and social studies. He had a three in drawing and manual arts and a three in music. His Japanese had gone up from a three to a four; otherwise, his grades were unchanged. In the comment section, Mr. Honda had written, "Kazuo was assistant leader of his class group and did a good job getting them organized and looking after everyone. In academics, he did his homework faithfully but could improve further with additional effort. Resist the temptation to be satisfied with the current results, and do your best."

Kazuo sighed. Mr. Honda had figured out that he hated to study.

When the students' cheers, dejected sighs, and surprised gasps had finally died down, the teacher spoke up.

"With that, we come to the end of the fall term. From tomorrow until January 7, we have winter vacation. Whatever you do, take good care of your health and try not to catch a cold. I look forward to seeing you all here in good spirits on January 8. Happy New Year."

The class bowed, and the term was over.

If this were a normal day, Kazuo would go with Nobuo, Nishino-kun, Minoru, and Yasuo to the empty lot and play awhile before going home. But when Kazuo went to peek into his brother's second-grade classroom, not a soul was in sight. Nobuo went right home, saying he had to help at the butcher shop, as they were selling the roasted chicken thighs for Christmas. Minoru left, too, explaining that he had to help his dad. That left Kazuo and Nishino-kun.

The two of them sat down on the dead grass in the empty lot and showed each other their report cards. Other than a five in drawing and manual arts, and a four in social studies, Nishino-kun had all threes.

"You got terrific grades," Nishino-kun told Kazuo. "Just once, I wish I could get a five in something other than drawing and manual arts."

Kazuo saw his friend sigh glumly. While Kazuo's grades were certainly better than Nishino-kun's, he thought that getting a five in drawing and manual arts, as Nishino-kun had done, was more impressive. Nishino-kun's drawings—like most of the thoughts in his head, for that matter—were completely different from everyone else's. When the class was sketching plants, the other students tried to make their drawings resemble the trees or grass or flowers they were looking at. But Nishino-kun's drawings didn't look a bit like what was in front him. If he was looking at a white flower with broad, flat leaves, he would put black lines in the flower and draw the leaves slightly twisted. But for some reason the plants he drew looked more alive than anyone else's.

"By the way, Nishino-kun, do you celebrate Christmas at your house?" Kazuo asked after he and Nishino-kun had finished sharing their report cards.

"Christmas? Not really. Mom will probably buy a Christmas cake, but we don't put up a Christmas tree or get presents or anything."

"I see." Kazuo was disappointed. He had faintly hoped that Nishino-kun's family would celebrate Christmas because they had so many foreign books. Then again, their house was so crammed with books they probably had no room for a Christmas tree. As far as Christmas went, it seemed Nishino-kun's family was no different from all the rest in West Ito.

"Well anyway, I'd better be getting home with these grades," Nishino-kun mumbled, sounding depressed.

Nishino-kun would probably get a talking-to from his

father. Thinking about it made Kazuo feel bad for his friend.

At his own house, Kazuo thought, he would have his own problems. Mother would come home from her job and say, "Kazuo, you know perfectly well that you could get better grades if you studied a little harder. Think about that over winter vacation and buckle down next term."

As for his father, he would probably work overtime again and come home late. Kazuo hoped that he would come straight home and not by way of Chujiya, the bar by the station. The last thing Kazuo wanted was to hear his drunken father rant, "Son, you are going to study harder and get into a national university, you hear me? Then you're going to get a Ph.D. and work at a top company. You're not going to have regrets and end up like me, got that?"

Soon, the two boys stood up and began to walk slowly down the roads that led to their houses.

That night Kazuo did get the usual talking-to from his mother when she came home from her job. But his father, who came home late after working overtime and stopping at the bar, was in extremely high spirits. He had bought a Christmas cake, which he placed on the *kotatsu*. Then he immediately fell asleep.

Sitting next to Father's snoring body, Kazuo, Yasuo, and Mother each enjoyed a slice of cake. Christmas was just one day, but tomorrow was the start of winter vacation—and that meant two whole weeks without having to think about school. Just the idea of it almost made Kazuo forget his grades, and that was a very good thing.

Winter Earnings

The first two days of winter vacation were pure heaven. Kazuo and Yasuo didn't have to go to school; their mother left home at eight in the morning and didn't return until five, and their father left even earlier, of course, and didn't come home until late. The middle part of the day, when both parents were away, was Kazuo and Yasuo's to spend pretty much as they pleased.

The TV stations were broadcasting special animated programs for children during winter vacation, so Kazuo and Yasuo stayed sprawled on their bedding all morning and watched TV. After that, they made instant ramen with cabbage and egg for lunch. When they had finished, they headed out to the empty lot to meet Nobuo or Nishino-kun or Minoru, and Kazuo continued training with Nobuo to run as fast as Bob Hayes, or they *sumo* wrestled with Minoru. Or they flew kites, even though it was a bit early for New Year's kite flying.

But the boys knew that their blissful freedom would come to an end soon.

New Year's

The period around New Year's Day, known as Oshogatsu, one of Japan's biggest and busiest holidays. People clean their houses and pay off their debts to get the new year off to a fresh start. Many travel to visit their families. There are shrine visits, decorations, special foods, lots of games, toys, and all kinds of seasonal events and TV shows. With children home from school and relatives around, most homes are full of bustle and noise.

Sukiyaki

A popular dish of meat simmered with vegetables and other ingredients in a slightly sweet broth of soy sauce and sugar. You prepare it at your own table using a pot on a gas burner. When the meat is done, you pick it out of the pot with chopsticks and dip it in a small bowl of raw, beaten egg.

That was because their father's company and the electronics factory where their mother worked both closed for **New Year's** vacation. On December 28, both parents would finish work earlier than usual. Mother would arrive home just after noon, and Father would be back around three.

On the morning of December 28, Kazuo and Yasuo's mother reminded them of something else.

"Kazuo, Yasuo. Uncle Yoshio is coming today, so don't mess up the house."

"Hooray, *sukiyaki* tonight!" exclaimed Yasuo, grinning widely.

Uncle Yoshio was their father's older brother. Each November he left the rural prefecture of **Yamagata**, where he lived, and came to Tokyo to work on construction sites to earn money for his family. This year he was helping to build a subway tunnel.

Once, during summer vacation, Kazuo and Yasuo had visited Uncle Yoshio's village, which was also where their father had been born. Surrounded by mountains, it was a quiet place with three clear streams meandering through its center. Spread out around the streams was a patchwork of flooded **paddy fields**. After dark, the fireflies that lived on the riverbanks filled the village with their tiny, faint lights, like dancing stars. For city kids like Kazuo and Yasuo, the sight was so beautiful it was like a dream.

The two of them had spent whole days outdoors with Takashi, the third of Uncle Yoshio's three sons and the closest to Kazuo in age, catching beetles in the mornings and swimming in the streams in the afternoons. At night, they would flop down on their bedding, worn out from play, and drift off to sleep while gazing at the fireflies. Takashi told them how beautiful it was in winter, too.

> **Yamagata**
> A prefecture (a bit like a state in America) in northern Japan, part of the rural Tohoku region along with Aomori, Fukushima, Iwate, and Miyagi prefectures. Known for farming, forestry, and fishing, Tohoku receives heavy snow every winter.

> **Paddy fields**
> Flooded areas of land used for growing rice. Rice paddies are found all over Asia. So numerous are they in Japan that 田, the original Japanese character for "field," comes from a drawing of a rice paddy.

"The snow piles up everywhere—the fields, the mountains—and everything turns completely white," he said. "It gets as high as a grown-up is tall, and we ski around on it and play every day. Have the two of you ever skied before?"

Kazuo and Yasuo shook their heads.

Listening to Takashi, Kazuo had wondered how Father could have left this gorgeous place and gone to Tokyo, which was crammed with people, buildings, and noise.

Then again, Uncle Yoshio's stories about his construction work were filled with thrills for Kazuo and Yasuo. He told them about how there was lots of water underground in the city. When workers constructed a building, they often pumped out enough water to fill dozens of swimming pools! And when construction crews were digging deep with cranes, they sometimes found people's dwellings from thousands of years ago.

The work at the construction sites stopped for New Year's vacation on December 28, and Uncle Yoshio always went back to his village to spend the New Year's holiday with his family. It had become a tradition for him to stop by Kazuo's house on the night of his departure. And the menu for dinner was always the same: *sukiyaki*.

"We'll keep the house clean," Kazuo promised as Mother headed out the front door.

"Hey, do you think Uncle Yoshio will bring us New Year's money?" Yasuo asked Kazuo.

"Maybe," Kazuo muttered as he carried his breakfast dishes to the kitchen. It wasn't that he didn't look forward

A Tokyo highway under construction in the mid-'60s.

to receiving New Year's money from Uncle Yoshio. He just felt that being open about it like Yasuo was childish.

"*Oi*, Yasuo, I'll do your dishes," Kazuo called to his brother, who remained seated at the *kotatsu*. "So bring them here."

> **Yakitori**
>
> Skewers of chicken and vegetables grilled and dipped or covered in sauce. Workers enjoy eating *yakitori* when meeting friends after work.

That afternoon their mother came home just after twelve, and their father came home at a little past three. Perhaps because of the upcoming six-day holiday, their expressions were milder than usual.

"Otohsan, why don't you take Kazuo and Yasuo to the bathhouse before your brother gets here?" Mother called from the kitchen, where she was starting to prepare dinner.

Father was in the living room playing thumb *sumo* with Kazuo and Yasuo. Today meant the end of their lazy days of freedom. But they had not seen much of Father for the past month while he worked overtime, and now they were having fun.

"All right, boys, we're off to the bathhouse," Father announced. Kazuo and Yasuo jumped to their feet.

With their towels and soap in their basins, Kazuo, Yasuo, and Father walked down the main street of the shopping area. A children's song, "Just a Few More Nights Till New Year's," blared from speakers. The shopping area was crowded with people stocking up on food for their New Year's celebrations. When Kazuo, Yasuo, and Father reached the center of the district, Yasuo's friend Nobuo, who was skewering chicken for **yakitori** at the back of his parents' butcher shop, noticed Kazuo and called out to him.

"Heading to the bathhouse early today, huh?"

Like his mother, who was frying croquettes and ground pork cakes at the front of the store, and his father, who was carving slabs of meat with a huge cleaver, Nobuo was wearing a white work smock over his clothes. Next to him, helping him slide pieces of chicken onto skewers, was Nobuo's older brother, Haruo.

"Yeah, Otohsan came home early," Yasuo said before Kazuo could respond.

"Kids shouldn't cut into other people's conversations," Kazuo said, giving Yasuo a poke in the face, then turned back to Nobuo. "Our uncle's coming tonight. We have orders to bathe before he gets here."

Nobuo winked. "So that's why your mom stopped by for *sukiyaki* beef a little while ago?"

"Guess so. You're helping the folks today?"

Nobuo nodded. "I'm working hard, that's for sure."

Nobuo's father looked up. "You're only doing this because I gave you a good talking-to, and because you want your New Year's money!" He flared his nostrils, looking exactly like his son, and Nobuo snickered.

"Our Kazuo and Yasuo haven't lifted a finger at home since the winter vacation started," Kazuo's father spoke up. "All they do is stare at the TV. They could learn a lot from your Nobuo." He put his hands on Kazuo's and Yasuo's heads and wagged them back and forth.

"Our boys only help every now and then," Nobuo's mother said, pausing as she turned a croquette. "What I wish is that they would study harder, like Kazuo-chan and Yasuo-chan."

"I guess the grass is always greener on the other side," Kazuo's father remarked.

The three adults laughed, and then exchanged formal, year-end greetings.

Later Kazuo, Yasuo, and Father returned from the bathhouse to find a portable burner and iron pot set out on the *kotatsu*. The hands of the clock showed it was past five.

"No sign of Yoshio yet?" Father asked Mother. Uncle Yoshio always arrived before five.

"No," Mother said. She stopped chopping the vegetables for *sukiyaki* and looked at Father with a worried expression.

"He's probably running late because they had a lot of work to do before New Year's," he told her. "Before we worry about that, why don't you go to the bathhouse. I can handle the rest of this."

"You're right. I'll be back."

Their mother left, and their father took over preparing the *sukiyaki* ingredients. He chopped onions, chrysanthemum greens, *shiitake* mushrooms, and tofu, piling them on plates, which Kazuo then carried to the living room. Yasuo took five *sukiyaki* bowls from the cupboard and set them out on the *kotatsu*.

"Do you know why there are so many vegetables in *sukiyaki*?" Father asked Kazuo and Yasuo, after they had laid everything out.

"Because if we only eat meat, it costs a lot of money?" Yasuo answered immediately.

Father laughed heartily. "Well, that's true. But that's not all there is to it. Kazuo, do you know?"

Aomori

A rural prefecture in north-eastern Japan, or Tohoku. Heavy snow historically led workers to warmer cities in winter to do seasonal labor.

"Um . . . for balanced nutrition?" Kazuo answered.

Father looked impressed. "Since when did you get to be such a smarty pants?"

Kazuo listened to his father explain to Yasuo how the vitamin C from vegetables helped people to stay healthy. Father knew things, just like a schoolteacher knew things, and sometimes he could explain math or science lessons even better than Mr. Honda. When Father had finished the chores in the kitchen, they resumed their rounds of thumb *sumo*. The three of them howled with laughter.

Finally, after their mother returned from the bathhouse, Uncle Yoshio arrived, carrying a bag stuffed with gifts for his family back home.

Uncle Yoshio always put everyone in a cheerful mood when he came to visit, telling jokes and fooling around. But today he heaved a sigh as he sank down at the *kotatsu*. "I'm sorry to be late," he murmured.

"What happened?" Father asked worriedly.

"A fellow named Toshi from upcountry in **Aomori** broke his leg. Getting him into the hospital and calling his people took all afternoon." Uncle Yoshio sighed again.

"Will Mr. Toshi be all right?" asked Kazuo's mother. She paused while lighting the burner to make the *sukiyaki*.

"The doctor says the bone should heal in a month, so everything will be fine. But it'll be at least March before poor old Toshi can work again." Uncle Yoshio shook his head and stared into the steam that rose from the *sukiyaki* pot. "And by then it'll be time to go home and get back in the fields. Basically, it means no income for him for the rest of the winter."

"Can't he get any compensation?" Father poured some beer into Uncle's glass.

"No. We're all just **seasonal labor**."

Uncle Yoshio sighed again and brought his glass to his mouth. "Here it is almost New Year's, and I come in with all this heavy talk. Sorry about that."

> **Seasonal labor**
>
> During the 1960s and later, when Japan was growing rapidly, some 200,000 to nearly 350,000 rural workers, among them people like Uncle Yoshio, migrated to cities each winter to find work. It was a hard life: families were separated, villages suffered, and workers were exposed to dangerous conditions (the incident involving Mr. Toshi shows some of the hazards of this work). The workers increasingly came from remote regions such as Tohoku, including Aomori and Yamagata prefectures.

"How is the job situation, by the way?" asked Father as he poured more beer into Uncle's glass to top it off.

"Last year there was a big construction rush because everyone was getting ready for the Olympics—putting up buildings and highways all over Tokyo. Now the Olympics are over so they're not hiring like they were. At least Tokyo doesn't have any snow, so a person can find some work. Back home in Yamagata, there's nothing to do all winter but shovel snow."

Father nodded.

"Hold on now," Uncle said suddenly, looking at Kazuo and Yasuo.

"I've been forgetting myself. Here, boys, this is for you."

He took two red New Year's envelopes from his shirt pocket and handed them to the boys.

"Wow, thanks!" Yasuo's eyes lit up as he received his.

Kazuo also expressed his thanks and put the small envelope in the pocket of his trousers.

"We thank you for your kindness every year," Mother said to Uncle Yoshio.

"Here, these are for Koichi-kun, Sanae-chan, and Takashi-kun." She took three envelopes from the chest of drawers and gave them to Uncle.

He bowed his head slightly, and then accepted the gifts with polite words of thanks.

"By the way, how is Takashi-kun?" Kazuo asked, remembering the cousin he had not seen in nearly two years.

"Takashi seems to be all right. The last letter I got from home said he's going to represent his school at a ski tournament in January." For the first time that day, Uncle's expression grew genuinely happy.

"Koichi-kun will be off to high school next year, won't he?" Mother asked, inquiring after Uncle's eldest son.

"That's right. He's studying hard, says he's going to take the exams for the top high school in the prefecture," Uncle responded proudly. "With that boy studying day and night, I've got to do my part and work just as hard."

A little later, just after nine, Uncle Yoshio stood up. He was getting ready to catch the overnight **train** to Yamagata from Ueno Station.

"Tomorrow morning I'll look out the window and the

whole world will be white!" He put his shoes on at the front door.

Father went to the station with Uncle to see him off.

After the men left, Mother began to clear off the *kotatsu*. Kazuo and Yasuo reluctantly withdrew from the *kotatsu*'s warmth, laid out the bedding in their small room, and curled up under their blankets.

> **Train**
>
> The entire archipelago of Japan is criss-crossed by train lines. Some are high-speed trains that link major cities; others are small and rickety wooden trains that journey deep into the mountains. In Kazuo's time few Japanese had their own cars but got around exclusively on train, streetcar, and subway.

"Hey, Niichan, how much New Year's money did you get?" Yasuo asked, poking his head out from under the covers.

"Five hundred yen," Kazuo answered shortly.

"Five hundred yen, huh? I got three hundred. Hey, what do you think you're going to buy with yours? A plastic model, or some comics maybe?"

"I haven't decided yet. You'd better get to sleep or we'll be in trouble." Kazuo pulled his covers over his head. In previous years, his mind would have been racing just like Yasuo's, thinking about what he would buy. But this year he kept thinking about how the gift had come from Uncle's hard, physical labor for the sake of his family. It was money earned from work that could have given him a broken leg, just like Mr. Toshi.

Kazuo turned over in his bedding. The only sound in the house was water running as their mother washed dishes. Father had not returned from the station yet.

Kazuo closed his eyes and remembered Uncle talking about the snow he would see tomorrow morning. Snow took away people's jobs in wintertime, and it was snow that his father had come to Tokyo to escape.

Even so, Kazuo couldn't help but hope that the snow his uncle saw in the morning would be glittering in the sunrise, its whiteness stretching as far as the eye could see.

First calligraphy of the New Year.

Yasuo's Big Mouth

To Kazuo, there was nothing quite as boring as New Year's. The adults created a formal atmosphere by wearing *kimono* for the first three days of the year, but it felt like there were a lot of limits on what children could do. Nobuo was off in the countryside in Shizuoka, where his parents came from, and most other families were either going out or receiving relatives who came to offer New Year's greetings. That meant Mother had strictly forbidden going to other children's houses or inviting any friends to their house to play.

From New Year's Eve through the third of January, the streets of Tokyo grew very quiet, as if all the people had disappeared.

Gone were the sounds of car engines running and tires squealing on the main roads, and of people's footsteps ceaselessly coming and going. Bells from far-off temples that were usually drowned out by noise suddenly became possible to hear, and the sky looked amazingly clean because nearly all of the factories were on holiday.

Kimono

Traditional Japanese garment worn by women, men, and children. *Kimono* are in the shape of a T and reach nearly to the floor. They have big collars and long, wide sleeves. *Kimono* don't use buttons. Instead they wrap across the front, the left side over the right. An *obi* (sash) wraps several times around the body and is tied in the back. When wearing a *kimono* you also put on split-toe socks and traditional footwear: either wooden or straw sandals. *Kimono* are usually worn by women, but rarely on a daily basis. Men may wear *kimono* at formal ceremonies. Young girls and unmarried women usually have very colorful *kimono* with bright designs.

On January 1, Kazuo's family ate a late breakfast of rice-dumpling soup and New Year's dishes. Then they exchanged greetings with other people in company housing, and paid their first visit of the year to a nearby shrine. On January 2, after Grandmother came over to spend some time and give New Year's money to Kazuo and Yasuo, they did their first **calligraphy** of the year. People said your writing would improve if you practiced calligraphy on January 2. But Kazuo had been doing it every year since he started grade school, and he couldn't see that his writing had improved even a little.

On January 3, there was absolutely nothing to do. Fortunately, some co-workers of Father's came over to toast the New Year, so Yasuo and Kazuo got to go to the empty lot to fly kites. There was hardly any wind, but some older kids were there, too. They were flying kites that had special New Year's expressions written on them.

Kazuo told Yasuo to hold their kite while he ran off with the string in his hand. He was trying to get the kite into the air by running to create an artificial wind. But when he slowed down even a little bit, the kite simply dropped to the ground, as if not in the mood.

The boys tried the same strategy several times, but the

kite showed no sign of staying up. And since it was made out of bamboo sticks and traditional paper, the edges tore every time it hit the ground. Soon it began to get dirty with mud. The boys finally gave up on kite flying and walked through the West Ito shopping area, where every store seemed to have closed its doors. There was not a soul to be seen in the street either.

"Oniichan, how come our kite wouldn't go in the air?" Yasuo asked grumpily. He was holding the kite, which by now was badly torn with its bamboo frame poking out.

"Because there's no wind, Yasuo."

"But those middle school kids got their kites up in the air. I wonder if we're just bad at it. Maybe we need an expensive kite, not a cheap old ten-yen kite."

"Yasuo, would you pipe down?" Kazuo said irritably. "Before we got there, they probably had a better wind than we did."

"We should've had Otohsan help us," Yasuo muttered.

Kazuo scowled. "You really can't shut your big mouth, can you? Anyway, Otohsan's busy today, so there's no way he can help." He stuffed his hands in his trouser pockets and continued walking through the quiet shopping area.

When they got to Takahashi Meats, Kazuo glanced at the floor above the butcher shop. He wondered if Nobuo's

---

Calligraphy

Traditional method of writing Japanese using a brush. There are several different ways of writing words and sounds: Chinese characters, or *kanji*; two phonetic scripts, *hiragana* and *katakana*, for writing syllables; and letters of the English alphabet. Numbers are usually written as 1, 2, 3, etc. Japanese schoolchildren know hundreds of *kanji* by the time they finish elementary school, and they learn them by writing them over and over. These days, many grown-ups are forgetting how to hand-write *kanji* (many of which have more than ten strokes) because the computer does it for them.

New Year's dishes

Traditional foods served at New Year's time throughout Japan. These *osechi* foods vary from region to region and are prepared before New Year's Eve so they will last through the holiday (until around January 3). They include kelp rolls, simmered black beans, mashed sweet potatoes with sweet chestnuts, candied dried sardines, fish cakes, and so on. Many people look forward to eating *osechi* at New Year's, much as Americans and Canadians look forward to Thanksgiving turkey and pumpkin pie.

family had come back from their visit to the country. But just as in the rest of the shopping area, there was no sign of any life, not even of Nobuo's older brother Haruo singing "*Ee-tsu bina hahdo deizu naito.*"

"Oh, hey, Niichan," Yasuo spoke up. "I wonder what we'll have for dinner tonight." He sniffed and rubbed his nose.

Right then, Kazuo felt that he couldn't take any more of Yasuo's chatter. That was because he knew exactly what Yasuo was trying to say. They were both sick of rice-dumpling soup and **New Year's dishes**.

Every year, after their family ate the traditional *soba* on New Year's Eve, they would eat nothing but rice-dumpling soup and special New Year's food, which had been boiled in soy sauce and sugar to keep it preserved, until the shops opened again on January 4 or 5. The soup and other dishes were tasty at first, but eating them three times a day for three days in a row soon made the boys long for regular food. Plus, the New Year's dishes they liked the best—sweetened fried egg and candied chestnut—were always completely gone by the time breakfast was over on January 1. Kazuo couldn't wait to have curry rice again, or a croquette, or even grilled fish.

"Look, if you can just put up with New Year's food for

one more day, we'll be back to regular food tomorrow," Kazuo now coolly observed. Yasuo's shoulders were slouched in disappointment.

At home, Father and his coworkers had just left. In the living room, the smell of beer and whiskey hung in the air.

"We're back." Kazuo and Yasuo took off their shoes and stepped into the room.

"Hey, cheese and ham!" Yasuo instantly spotted leftover food on a plate on the *kotatsu*. "Okaasan, where did this come from?"

"That's so unfair! We go away and the adults eat all this good stuff by themselves," Kazuo said. He beat Yasuo to the plate and ate some cheese.

"Hey, Oniichan! I want some, too!" Yasuo grabbed some cheese of his own and shoved it into his mouth.

"What are you two doing? That'll be quite enough funny business on New Year's." Mother warned, coming out of the kitchen while drying her wet hands. She was wearing a special white apron over her *kimono*.

"But Oniichan tried to eat before I did!"

"Oh, be quiet. You're the one who can't stop talking and driving me crazy." Kazuo lightly knocked his brother on the head.

Mother frowned. "No more fighting, boys. Kazuo, you're the older one, so you'd better set a good example. And boys, you may eat the cheese and ham. But I want you to sit down properly and eat it with these, not with your hands." Mother handed them some small forks that were used to eat fruit.

"I always have to be the one who gets in trouble," Kazuo muttered grumpily. He quickly speared a thinly sliced piece of ham with his fork and brought it to his mouth.

"This food was something we had set aside for guests," Mother said. "I haven't had any of it yet myself, and it was purchased with your father's hard-earned money. So it needed to go to his visitors first." She put the single remaining piece of cheese in her mouth.

"All we get every day is rice-dumpling soup and New Year's dishes. We like ham and cheese, too!" Yasuo said.

"Be grateful for what you have, Yasuo. During the war, we got a single, tiny rice dumpling and a single tangerine on January 1. I remember wishing I could eat rice-dumpling soup and New Year's dishes until my stomach was bursting! But we couldn't have any special New Year's dishes, and I was grateful just to have that rice dumpling and tangerine."

Oh boy, thought Kazuo. His eyes met Yasuo's. Their mother was going to talk about "during the war" again. But just then they heard their father's voice.

"Hey, boys, you're back," he called. "What's wrong with the three of you, looking all long-faced on New Year's?" Father slid into the *kotatsu*.

"The boys were complaining that they're tired of soup and New Year's food, and I was telling them how important it is to be grateful for the food they have," Mother said. She stared irritably at Father, whose face was flushed from drinking with his friends.

He shrugged. "Well, New Year's food does get old when you eat it for three days straight."

"What's this?" She scowled. "You're taking their side now?"

"Come on, don't get upset," he told her. "Today's the last day of the New Year's holiday, so why don't we go to Shibuya or someplace for dinner? The department stores should be open by now."

"All *right*!" Kazuo and Yasuo jumped up, but Mother's face was still angry.

"Hold on, now. Here I am trying to teach the boys about gratitude for the food they have, and you come in saying let's go out to eat?"

"What you say is perfectly right, my dear. We mustn't forget to be grateful for our food. But last year, I worked overtime practically every day and could never take these boys anywhere. It's the last day of New Year's. Surely we can do a little something special for them."

At first, Mother made no move to change her sullen expression. But Kazuo and Yasuo stared at her pleadingly. Finally, she nodded her head.

Shibuya, now all decked out to welcome the New Year, was one of Kazuo and Yasuo's favorite areas in Tokyo. Kazuo thought it was extremely modern and exciting. Four elevated railroad lines—the Kokuden, Ginza, Toyoko, and Inogashira lines—ran from Shibuya Station in four different directions.

To Kazuo, Shibuya looked exactly like a city of the future you would see in science fiction shows on TV. But Mother, who had lived in Shibuya as a girl, complained that you could no longer see the old face of the city.

Yasuo loved to see the bronze statue of the Akita dog named Hachiko outside of Shibuya Station. Years before, the real Hachiko had waited and waited here for his master to return home, even after he had died suddenly from illness. The story of the faithful Hachiko had been memorialized by the statue and was a favorite of Yasuo's. So as soon as they left the west exit, Yasuo went bounding through the crowds to stand in front of Hachiko. The black-colored statue sat, as always, on a pedestal with its eyes trained on the goings-on in Shibuya. Kazuo and his parents could tell from behind that Yasuo was speaking to the dog. When he had finished, he gave a deep bow.

"Yasuo, what did you ask Hachiko for?" Mother asked as Yasuo rejoined the family.

"Huh? Oh, nothing," Yasuo said.

"I know. You asked for your chatter-itis to finally heal this year, didn't you?" Kazuo said, poking fun at his brother.

"I did not," Yasuo said. He made a face at Kazuo. "Actually, I asked for a very nice older brother who would never tease and make fun of me."

"You're going to get it now!" Kazuo said, acting furious and raising a fist.

"Okaasan, help me! Oniichan's picking on me!" Yasuo hid behind Mother.

"Stop it this instant, you two. We'll have no more fighting on New Year's," Mother said sharply. "Kazuo, if I've told you once, I've told you a thousand times: You're the older one, so no picking on your brother."

"You'd better shape up now, boys," Father added. "We've come all this way to Shibuya for dinner, so put on your best behavior in front of other people. Got it?" It was rare for Father to warn them about their behavior. Kazuo and Yasuo nodded obediently.

Kazuo and his family matched their pace to the slowly moving crowds around them as they walked. Yasuo held onto Mother's hand and chattered on about all sorts of trivial things.

"Okaasan, when you were little, did you like summer or winter vacation better? I like winter because we don't have to do any homework. But school's going to start up again in four more days, isn't it? That's really soon.

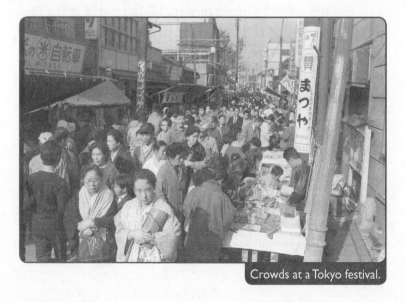

Crowds at a Tokyo festival.

"Okaasan, you were living in Shibuya, right? So did you ever meet Hachiko?"

Yasuo was happy to be walking along holding Mother's hand, Kazuo realized. Yasuo was finally getting to spend as much time as he wanted with Mother, who was often working.

Kazuo stuck both hands into the pockets of his overcoat and walked along silently next to his father.

Soon, they saw the sign for a restaurant called Suzuran. Kazuo always ordered **curry rice** when they went there.

In Kazuo's opinion, the curry rice at Suzuran was no ordinary curry rice. That was because the curry at Suzuran was served in a separate silver container, which Kazuo felt was very impressive.

But the tables at Suzuran were all full today, and a line had formed outside the restaurant. Father went inside to see how long the wait would be.

"An hour at the earliest, they said. Plus they have reduced hours for the holiday, so they're closing at five thirty." It was already four thirty.

"Let's find someplace else," Father said.

The family began to walk around Shibuya looking for another place to eat. But every restaurant was full. It wasn't until the fourth place they tried, a small cafe far from the station, that they were able to get in. It was certainly not very clean. The plastic tabletops had cigarette burn marks here and there, and the chairs were round stools with cotton stuffing coming out of the cushions. Even so, perhaps because it was New Year's, the restaurant was full of customers.

Mother, Father, Kazuo, and Yasuo were shown to a table in a corner.

"I wonder if this place will be any good," Kazuo said anxiously to Father.

"You know, sometimes it's these holes in the wall that actually have the good food," Father told him, smiling.

But when he looked at the menu, his face registered dismay. "Special New Year's Menu Today. Dinner: Curry rice or breaded pork on rice, 250 yen. Dessert: Soda water or ice cream, 150 yen."

Mother frowned, too. "My, this is expensive, isn't it?"

"Well, nothing we can do about it now," Father said. "What are you boys going to have?"

"Curry rice," they both answered without hesitation.

"Really? Well, then, why don't we all have that," Father told them and ordered four from the waitress.

"What did I tell you?" Mother complained to him after the waitress had left.

"Now, now, it might be good curry. Let's wait and see what they bring us."

No matter how disgusting or expensive this curry rice might be, Kazuo and Yasuo were certain it would taste better than the rice-dumpling soup and salty-sweet dishes they had been eating for days. They nodded at their father's words.

But Mother continued to grumble as Kazuo looked

again at the menu and tried to imagine what the "Special New Year's Menu" curry rice would be like.

If the curry was special for the holiday, it should have a lot of meat in it. And the rice and curry would probably be in separate containers, so he could pour the curry sauce a little at a time from its silver vessel onto the rice. But as Kazuo was daydreaming about the food, the bustling restaurant suddenly went quiet.

He looked around.

Sitting at the next table, which had been vacant until a moment before, was an older couple.

At first glance, they looked like a typical husband and wife in their sixties. Both had white hair. The man wore a light brown suit with a necktie, and the woman wore a two-piece winter dress. But when Kazuo gazed more closely at her, a soft "ah" escaped his lips. Then he instantly looked down at his lap, embarrassed.

The woman was cradling a doll, a large doll about the size of a two-year-old child. Its cloth face was stained, and its hair, which was closely cropped like a boy's, had lost its luster and shape. It was dressed in a white cotton outfit, like real toddlers wore, and it even had on a thick, light green overcoat.

Kazuo had seen similar couples on trains and in restaurants. They were often in their sixties, like this couple, and the wife would be holding a doll the size of a real baby. Her husband would be sitting quietly beside her. Kazuo knew that these were couples who had lost a child in the war.

When the child had died, either in battle or in an air raid at home, the shock had caused psychological harm to the wife. The husband had given her the doll as a way of calming her. To the woman in the restaurant today, the doll in her arms was the real child who still lived in her memories.

As his parents were doing, Kazuo behaved as though he hadn't seen the couple next to him. The gentleman quietly ordered curry rice for two from the waitress. Soon, the conversations in the restaurant started up again. Father and Mother dropped their argument and began to talk about how business was looking for Father's company this year. Kazuo drank his water, working as hard as he could not to glance to the side. Then he turned toward Yasuo to see if his brother had noticed the doll. He'd assumed that Yasuo would also be carefully looking away from the older couple at the neighboring table.

But he was wrong.

Instead, Yasuo was gazing with deep interest at the doll in the older woman's arms.

"*Oi*, Yasuo, you better quit it," Kazuo said softly, pulling on his brother's sweater.

Yasuo looked back at Kazuo.

Father also noticed Yasuo staring at the doll. "By the way, Yasuo," he asked abruptly. "What is your resolution for this year?"

"Huh, resolution? What's a resolution?" Yasuo turned toward Father.

"A resolution is something you would like to work on

this year. For example, studying thirty minutes every day so you'll get better at schoolwork. Or practicing running so you can go faster."

"Mmm . . . I don't know. I would like to have a dog," Yasuo said finally.

"It's not like making a wish, Yasuo," Father told him, smiling. "It involves something you want to work toward and be able to do."

"Umm, I'll tell you later," Yasuo said, looking back at the couple next to them again.

"Yasuo, you mustn't stare all around you that way," Mother said in a soft but firm voice. "Nobody likes to have people watching them while they eat."

"Your mother's right, Yasuo," added Father. "In this kind of place, the most important thing is to be polite and wait patiently for your food. Do you understand?" Kazuo thought that Father and Mother probably wanted to explain to Yasuo why the grown woman next to them was clasping a doll so lovingly. But they couldn't do that now, while the couple could hear them.

Yasuo's such a baby, Kazuo thought as he sipped water from his cup. He doesn't understand the concept of considering people's feelings.

Soon, their curry rice was brought out. The moment he saw it, Kazuo was disappointed. First, the curry was not in a separate container after all, but had been ladled directly onto the rice. Second, nowhere in the curry was there anything that looked like meat. Third, the dish did not even give off the pleasant aroma of curry.

"Let's eat up before it gets cold," Father said, picking up his spoon.

They all brought the meatless curry to their mouths silently. The only sound was the scrape of their spoons against their dishes.

Rice-dumpling soup and New Year's food would have been much better than this, Kazuo thought.

"Yasuo!" Mother whispered.

Kazuo looked at Yasuo.

> **Noh**
>
> Classical Japanese theater. The stage is bare, with just a pine tree painted on a wood-panel background. There are only a few actors, each wearing a long robe and usually a stylized wooden mask. The pace is slow, and the themes tend to be religious and tragic, compared to Kabuki, which is much more flashy and full of rich humor and adventure.

His brother had stopped moving his spoon and was staring at the doll.

"Say, ma'am?" Yasuo suddenly addressed the woman next to them.

Kazuo was stunned. So were his parents. And they were all terrified that Yasuo was about to ask one simple question: "Why are you holding that doll?"

"Say, ma'am," he said again. "What's your little boy's name?"

For a moment, everybody froze. That was the last thing they had expected Yasuo to say.

The woman, whose face had been as empty and expressionless as a **Noh** mask, blinked in surprise. "His name?" she echoed. Her voice sounded tender and fragile.

"Yes, his name." Heedless of the woman's bewilderment, Yasuo began to chat. "My name is Yasuo. Yasuo Nakamoto. And the person next to me is my older brother Kazuo, and here are my father Koji and my mother Yoshiko. We all have names, see? So I was wondering what the name of your little boy is."

"My boy's . . . name . . . " murmured the woman. She gently stroked the head of the doll held to her chest. Then Kazuo saw her smile. "Toru."

"Oh, Toru-kun, I see." Yasuo repeated her son's name and went on to say that he was a second-grader at West Ito Elementary School and that he liked math and science but hated social studies and music. Then he continued talking about all sorts of other things.

Father turned to the woman's husband. "I'm so sorry. Our son is a real chatterbox."

"Not at all, there's no need to apologize," the man said quietly. A faint smile played on his lips. "Indeed, I should be thanking you. It has been a very long time since I have seen my wife look happy."

He gazed at his wife as she listened to Yasuo.

"We don't have many opportunities to talk to people, even when we go out. I suppose everybody thinks they should leave us in peace. For my wife, having your little boy talk to her is a real treat. I must thank you." The man took a drink of water from his cup.

"Did you lose a son in the war?" Mother asked hesitantly.

"Yes, our boy died in the fighting at Guadalcanal. He was an only child, who we were blessed with after years of waiting, so the official notice of death came as a great shock to my wife. Somehow we've managed to keep going for these twenty years. Now, when I look at my wife, quietly living within her memories, I get the feeling she might be a lot better off than I am."

Kazuo laughed uneasily though he didn't know exactly what the man meant. The man, who had neatly combed hair, removed his glasses and lightly rubbed his eyes with his fingertips.

Kazuo watched as Father and Mother nodded deeply at the man's words.

The train on the way home was nearly empty. In their car, which had no one in it except for the four of them, Kazuo sat on the long bench under the window with his family and gazed out at the tiny lights moving past.

"I wonder what will become of that couple," Mother said with a sigh.

"Who knows?" Father answered. "They'll probably go through old age just the way they are."

"Probably," she said, sighing again. Then she added her usual pet phrase: "I am sick and tired of war."

"*Oi*, Yasuo," Kazuo said to his brother, who was being unusually quiet as he watched the nighttime scenery. "Did you know all the time why that lady was holding the doll?"

"Of course I did," Yasuo answered, tilting his head slightly toward Kazuo.

"Then why did you ask its name?" Father wanted to know.

Yasuo shrugged. "Because the lady looked so lonely.

And you know me," he added with a sly grin. "I like to talk!"

"That's for sure!" exclaimed Kazuo, and everyone laughed. Then once again Kazuo turned to the bright city lights that were streaming by. Maybe Yasuo wasn't as much of a child as he'd thought, Kazuo reflected.

Kazuo silently wished his family, and that white-haired couple, a happy New Year. Another year had come upon them, and things were already changing, right before his eyes.

Keiko Sasaki

Kazuo loved American cartoons and dramas. That was because they showed a lot of different people living wealthy lifestyles. But there was one thing that bothered him about these shows: they had a lot of kissing in them.

In *Leave It to Beaver*, for example, the father and mother kissed when the father went to work. They kissed again when he came home. In *Popeye*, Bluto tried to get the unwilling Olive to kiss him, and when Popeye ate some spinach and defeated Bluto, Popeye and Olive puckered up their lips like fish and glued them together, making a big, wet sucking sound. No matter what show it was, if it was from America and had a man and a woman in it, it almost always ended with the man passionately kissing the woman.

It wasn't that Japanese TV shows didn't have kissing. They did, but only in dramas for adults, like the shows Kazuo saw his mother watching when he happened to be awake after nine o'clock. And whenever a kissing scene came on, Mother quickly said, "It's late! Time for children to be in bed!" and chased him off to his room. Kazuo understood, of course, that kissing was something grown-ups who liked each other tended to do. But he wasn't convinced that he would ever kiss anybody when he grew up. Kissing meant that some other person's spit would end up in his mouth. He also thought that kissing was something you should do hidden away from other people, not right in front of them.

Kazuo's mother and father had never kissed in front of Kazuo or Yasuo. But Kazuo had seen them kiss once. That was when he was in second grade and woke up in the middle of the night.

At that time, all four members of the family were still sleeping together in the six-mat living room. When Kazuo happened to wake up in the dark one night, he noticed that his father and mother were gone and that one of the sets of bedding was missing. Slipping out of his blankets, he slid open the papered door to the four-and-a-half-mat room and peered in. And there he saw the missing set of bedding, and his father and mother embracing and kissing inside it. Kazuo, who had never seen his parents kiss, was startled and hurried back to his own bedding. He pulled his blanket over his head, and held very still until he finally fell back asleep.

And now, whenever he was watching TV and saw a kissing scene, he would get a heavy feeling in the pit of his stomach. He didn't know whether the same thing happened to Yasuo, and he had never asked Nobuo, Nishino-kun, or Minoru whether it happened to them.

At school, Kazuo also did his best not to show any

interest in the girls in his class. This was not difficult for Ka-zuo, because hanging out with his friends was much more fun than chatting with the girls, who talked nonstop. Just one girl in his class, Keiko Sasaki, seemed to weigh on his mind. It wasn't that Kazuo didn't like Keiko Sasaki. He just didn't like the particular way other people looked at him when he was with her.

Keiko Sasaki's father was an employee at Nihon Optics, just like Kazuo's father, and her family lived in the same company housing compound as Kazuo's family. Keiko's family was made up of her father, her mother, herself, and a younger sister who would turn three this year. If you left out the fact that both children in her family were girls, the family make-up was exactly the same as Kazuo's. But Kazuo often got the feeling that Keiko's family was the exact opposite of his.

Keiko's father was a quiet, small man who neither drank alcohol nor smoked. Kazuo's father was tall and liked beer. Father did not speak ill of Mr. Sasaki; he said he was "not a bad man, just a little strange." Keiko's mother was short like her husband, and never raised her voice to scold Keiko or her little sister, Yasuko. According to Mother, that was because Keiko and her sister were good children who listened care-fully to what their parents said, unlike a certain pair of broth-ers who never did what they were told.

Finally, Keiko was an excellent student—so good that she was probably number one or two in Kazuo's class. She was good at all subjects, unlike Kazuo who had definite strong and weak areas. And Keiko was one of the prettier girls. Her skin was creamy and her eyes were large. And she was nice to everybody in the class, so there was no one, boy or girl, who said anything bad about her.

Kazuo had been buddies with Keiko until shortly after they started grade school. They had played together almost every day. And early on in grade school, they had walked to and from school together. But in their class was a group of students who made fun of their friendship and started calling them "husband and wife." Kazuo did not like this, and began to steer clear of Keiko. And Keiko, perhaps because she knew Kazuo was being teased, began to act distant toward him as well.

That was why Kazuo felt uncomfortable about Keiko. And when, at the beginning of November, Mr. Honda had made them part of the same class group—with Keiko the leader and Kazuo the assistant leader—Kazuo had secretly worried about being called "husband and wife" again. But Keiko, perhaps because she remembered the events of first grade, spoke no more than was necessary to Kazuo. In fact, she acted rather indifferent toward him, just as he did to her, so that they never heard any teasing from their classmates.

And Kazuo had been relieved by that.

Winter vacation ended, and the final term of the school year began. Kazuo did not particularly like this part of the school year. Perhaps it was because the **weather** was at its coldest in January. The north wind kicked up and barreled through town, churning up dust and making the hands of Kazuo and his playmates as dry as sandpaper. Still, Kazuo kept rounding up Minoru and Nishino-kun, and doing his Bob Hayes training with Nobuo at the empty lot, and playing *sumo*, or leapfrog, or kick-the-stone, or baseball. Soon his body would warm up, and he would forget about the cold.

The weather in Tokyo is very similar to that of Washington, D.C. on the east coast of the United States: cold in the winter, hot and humid in the summer, and very pleasant in the spring and fall. Lacking central heating and air conditioning, however, most Japanese homes like Kazuo's were not very comfortable when the weather outside was extreme.

Weather

But that was not how it was in the classroom, where you couldn't run around. Mr. Honda lit the coal stove ten minutes before first period began, but not even he could always get it to light quickly. Sometimes, the stove would fill with smoke, and all the smoke that did not fit into the stove-pipe would puff out into the classroom.

"Everyone, I know you're cold, but please open the windows for a short time," Mr. Honda would tell them, an apologetic expression on his face.

Even colder air would pour in and make the children shiver all the more. On those days, the classroom might not warm up until the morning sunlight hit the windows directly, sometime after eleven a.m.

About two weeks into this frigid term, Kazuo and the other students in his class were back in their small groups. They were organizing the results of some science experiments, writing their findings on large pieces of paper.

The theme chosen by Kazuo's group was, "Do people have dark shadows and light shadows?" They had chosen this based on a question posed by Nishino-kun, who had said,

"What do they mean when they talk about people with light shadows? Is there really such a thing?" Students in the other groups had chosen questions more appropriate to science class, such as why shadows get longer in the winter or why certain trees' leaves change color. But for some reason, Kazuo's group had gone along with one of the strange thoughts whirling around inside Nishino-kun's head.

When Mr. Honda first heard their question, he looked a little surprised.

"Well, the point of science is to raise questions about all sorts of things and go after the answers," he said, then smiled.

For about a week, the members of Kazuo's group stared at the shadows of the classmates, upperclassmen, and underclassmen playing in the schoolyard during lunch recess and after school. What they learned was that there was no difference in how dark people's shadows were, other than the differences caused by changes in the weather. In other words, everybody's shadow was dark on sunny days and light on partly cloudy days, and almost invisible on completely overcast days. A strong light was needed in order to make dark shadows, so Kazuo's group concluded that an expression like "people with light shadows" described people who just didn't make much of an impression.

At first, Kazuo thought this was an odd topic to research and only did it to go along with Nishino-kun, but he was eventually impressed at how making some observations had led them to an interesting discovery.

Keiko seemed impressed, too. "You think up a lot of interesting things, don't you, Nishino-kun?"

She opened her round, black eyes wide at Nishino-kun, who was deftly drawing a person and his shadow on their group's piece of paper.

"Really, you think so?" Nishino-kun blushed a little.

Kazuo suddenly wondered if his friend had a crush on Keiko. He found himself envying the red-faced Nishino-kun a little because of the way his feelings showed. If it were Kazuo, and Keiko had spoken to him that way, Kazuo would probably have acted all gruff and just let her comment go by. Maybe that meant that he himself had a crush on Keiko.

He stole a glance at the side of her face, where some hair had escaped her barrette. She was still talking to Nishino-kun and didn't notice Kazuo studying her. He caught himself and quickly looked away.

Every day, the weather grew colder. The chill of the early morning was particularly harsh, and there were times when the pipes would freeze and water wouldn't come out of the kitchen faucet. Mother would put water in the kettle at night before sleeping, and in the morning, she'd boil it and pour it over the frozen faucet.

When morning came, Kazuo and Yasuo stayed curled up in their blankets like hibernating bears. But soon, their mother would come in and demand, "How long are you planning to stay in there?" Then she would strip off their blankets, exposing their bodies to the winter cold in one fell swoop.

Frost began to form on the dirt road that ran in front

of company housing, and when they walked to school, it would crunch beneath their feet, sounding like wafers being chewed. Maybe because the temperature dropped so quickly, a number of students at school got sick. One day, five in Kazuo's class stayed home due to illness.

"Everyone, this is your final term in fourth grade. Please take care and don't get sick," Mr. Honda said after lighting the coal stove. "To avoid catching a cold, you should wash your hands regularly. Gargling also helps to rid your body of germs from the air that are trying to get into your system." The teacher drew a picture of a human body on the chalkboard and drew a circle around the nose and throat.

"The next most important thing is to go to bed early and focus on maintaining a good diet. And after you bathe at night, be sure to bundle up in bed as soon as possible. I know

Tooth-brushing exercises at a Shinagawa Ward elementary school.

that a number of you go to public baths, as I do. I encourage you to go right home without stopping anywhere along the way."

Mr. Honda wrote the following on the chalkboard:

> Wash hands
> Gargle
> Early to bed and early to rise
> Eat three meals a day
> Stay warm after bathing

Wow, Mr. Honda goes to a public bath, too, Kazuo thought. For some reason, that made him feel terrific. Maybe the bath where Mr. Honda went also had a big mural of Mount Fuji. Kazuo was much more interested in hearing about Mr. Honda's bathhouse than in learning about colds. But Mr. Honda said nothing further on the subject and instead started their Japanese lesson.

That afternoon, the north wind blew harshly through the streets, whistling like an out-of-tune flute. After he said good-bye to his friends at the empty lot, Kazuo hurried home with Yasuo. The dark house was as chilly as the outdoors. The boys turned on the light in the living room and then hit the switch on the *kotatsu* so they could stick their frozen legs and arms underneath and warm up. Soon, Kazuo went to the kitchen and put rice and water in the electric rice cooker and pushed the switch.

In the past, Mother had cooked the morning and evening rice in a special pot that sat on a gas burner, but after

Father got his company bonus, they'd purchased an automatic rice cooker. Now, Kazuo and Yasuo were trading off days, preparing the rice for dinner.

When boiling it the old way, with the pot cooking on gas, it was difficult to get the strength of the flame just right. Mother would always recite, "First it flickers, then it pops. Keep the lid on, or it flops!" But with the electric rice cooker, all they had to do was wash the rice, put it in, and add water. So both Kazuo and Yasuo could do it easily.

After Kazuo had finished preparing the rice, the man from Imamura Tofu came into the neighborhood. Kazuo went out to buy some, and by the time he got back, Yasuo was watching an American cartoon that starred two magpies, Heckle and Jeckle, while copying his Japanese characters for school.

Kazuo sat next to him, pulled his math books from his backpack, and began to review his lessons.

Kazuo and Yasuo did their homework, laughing out loud at the antics of the two magpies, who were naughty and arrogant and constantly committing funny blunders. Mother did not come back until after five thirty.

"Did you get your homework done?" That was her first question for Kazuo and Yasuo, who by now were completely tucked into the *kotatsu* and intently watching *Good Golly Gourd Island*, the puppet drama that came on at five forty-five..

"Yep!" The two of them proudly held up their notebooks, not mentioning that they'd done their homework in front of the TV.

If she had been there earlier, she would have nagged them: "Study in front of the TV and you won't remember a single, solitary thing."

"Well, all right then," she said today, and then went into the kitchen and began to prepare dinner.

> An American comedy act of the early to mid-20th century featuring the slapstick and antics of three dimwits: Moe, Larry, and Curly. Their short films were broadcast in Japan from 1963 to 1967.
>
> **The Three Stooges**

Father had said he would be late again tonight due to overtime. When he was late, dinner was always very plain. But Kazuo and Yasuo knew better than to say anything about it, because their mother was sure to start in about "during the war." Also, if she got in a bad mood, their TV-watching time after dinner could be affected. So the boys ate the dried fish and stewed vegetables without a word, then turned on the TV.

Their favorite American comedy, *The Three Stooges,* was already underway. On the screen, the short one, Moe, was talking boastfully in a loud voice to block-headed Curly and forgetful Larry. Moe strutted back and forth, too caught up in what he was saying to notice Curly eating a banana, then throwing the peel on the floor.

As anyone would expect, Moe suddenly slipped on the banana peel and fell flat on his back. He flailed around with exaggerated movements that made the guests in the studio audience guffaw. Kazuo and Yasuo also laughed loudly.

But that was as far as their fun went.

"Okay, boys, I want you to go to the bath now," Mother said. She was using that tone of voice that meant she would not tolerate any argument.

Still Yasuo stuck out his lower lip. "How come? We're watching *The Three Stooges*."

"I don't care whether you're watching *The Three Stooges* or *The Two Stooges*, you are going to the bathhouse." With that, she reached over and switched off the TV.

"But Fujita Yu is closed today," Kazuo said, remembering that today was the second Thursday of the month, when the bath was always closed.

"Of course Fujita Yu is closed today." She swatted Kazuo's hand away as he reached toward the TV. "So today you will go to Hikari Yu. It's a little bit farther, but if you go right now, you should be back around eight. Okay?" She held out their basins.

Kazuo sighed. There was no choice but to listen obediently to her and go to the bath. Still, he didn't like bathing at Hikari Yu. The tubs were only half as big as the tubs at Fujita Yu, and the mural of Mount Fuji was so puny that it seemed pitiful.

"There's a cold going around right now," Mother went on, tying mufflers around their necks. "So before you get out of the tub, you absolutely must get in up to your shoulders and count to one hundred. And once you are out, dry your bodies and your hair well, and come straight home without dawdling. And Yasuo, Hikari Yu is smaller than Fujita Yu, so no playing Gourd Island in the big tub." She had spotted the model of Gourd Island that Yasuo had hidden between the towels in his basin, and removed it.

By the time Kazuo and Yasuo arrived at Hikari Yu, it was a quarter after seven. When they entered the changing area, they smelled cedar mixed with steam—the special odor of the bathhouse. The bathing area, separated from the changing room by a glass door, had only five or six people inside.

Before taking a Japanese bath, you completely wash your body outside the tub, soaping up and scrubbing vigorously, and then rinsing. After that, you go into the tub just to soak. In Japan, you *never* soap up in the tub and *never* bring your towel into the tub.

Scrubbing

Yasuo tossed his clothing into a bamboo basket and frowned as he looked around. "I bet everybody else is at home right now watching *The Three Stooges*."

"Nothing we can do about that, and you know it. Be a man and hurry up." Kazuo figured Yasuo was more upset about having his Gourd Island model taken away than about missing *The Three Stooges*.

Urging Yasuo along, Kazuo headed to the bathing area holding his basin with the soap and hand towel inside.

The bathing area was filled with hot, humid air. They sat at a faucet near the center of the **scrubbing** area, which consisted of three rows of faucets. They poured hot water over themselves till they were warm, then rubbed soap on their towels and scrubbed themselves from head to toe. They could feel the pores all over their bodies gradually opening after being shut tight against the cold outdoors.

"Hey, Niichan." Yasuo poked Kazuo in the side. "Isn't that Keiko-chan over there?" Yasuo jerked his jaw toward a faucet to their right. Through the steam Kazuo could see the back of a short man who had two girls with him.

It was not unusual for girls to be brought into the men's bath by their fathers. Kazuo had been taken into the women's bath by his mother until early in first grade. When his class-mates began to tease him, he went to the men's side.

But Keiko Sasaki was a fourth-grader just like Kazuo. Would a girl in fourth grade really come into the men's bath, even with her father? Figuring Yasuo must be seeing things, Kazuo peered through the steam at the three figures. Immediately next to the man sat a tiny girl with a short, bobbed haircut, and next to her was a bigger girl whose hair was a bit longer. Perhaps because the two girls had just finished washing their hair, it was wet and gleamed dark black.

Kazuo looked closely at the profile of the girl who sat on the end. Her hair fell to her pale shoulders, and he could just make out large eyes and thin lips. Perhaps because of the steam in the bathing area, her cheeks were slightly pink. She looked different than Keiko normally looked, but those eyes and lips were definitely hers.

The instant he realized the girl was Keiko Sasaki, his heart began to beat so forcefully that he thought it might stop completely.

I shouldn't look! He quickly averted his eyes from her and her family. Looking at the floor, he continued to scrub his body with his soapy towel.

"I wonder why Keiko-chan and her sister are here," Yasuo said innocently.

Not answering, Kazuo continued to look down and scrub.

"Hey, Niichan, let's wash each other's backs," Yasuo said.

"Not tonight. Let's each do our own." Kazuo didn't want Yasuo to sense the unease in his body.

"Why? You're weird," Yasuo told him. Then he washed up by himself and headed to the main tub. Kazuo remained alone at his faucet, slowly continuing to wash. The soap he had first rubbed on his towel was almost completely gone now, so he rubbed on some more, his hand trembling a little.

Good grief, what's wrong with me? he thought, growing irritated with himself for getting so nervous.

At last, Kazuo saw from the corner of his eye that Keiko's family was leaving the washing area for the changing room. Her body, as she stood up, was white and slender, and looked a little like a small fish.

As soon as her family disappeared, he breathed a huge sigh of relief. Then he poured basins full of water over himself to wash away the soap bubbles plastered all over him.

The next morning, when he and Yasuo left the house for school, Kazuo saw Keiko standing at the entrance to company housing. He took a big breath and tried to walk casually by her.

"Nakamoto-kun." Keiko spoke to Kazuo as he passed.

He stopped in his tracks and looked at her. He could see that she wanted to tell him something.

"*Oi*, Yasuo, you go on ahead." After sending Yasuo on his way, Kazuo stood in front of Keiko and kicked a pebble around. "Was there something you needed?"

"It's about yesterday." Keiko spoke softly and didn't look

at him. "My mother had a cold and my father needed me to help look after Yasuko, so I went because I had to."

"Okay, got it." He avoided meeting her eyes, concentrating on his feet instead. "You don't have to worry about me saying anything. I don't chatter on and on like girls do."

"Thanks." She smiled, showing her white teeth. Then she began to walk off to school, her back straight as always.

He sighed a little as he watched her go. He found himself wishing that he had looked just a little more at her white, fish-like body. But when he considered that he had intentionally decided not to look at her, he felt much better.

Who in his right mind tenses up when seeing a body that looks like a fish anyway? he thought a second later. The racing of his heart yesterday might have been just a dream. He laughed to himself and kicked the pebble at his feet again.

Then, thinking he would catch up with Yasuo, he ran as fast as he could down the road to school.

Kazuo's Typical Tokyo Saturday

Every once in a while, Kazuo liked to walk around his part of Tokyo by himself. He would get in the mood to ramble without Yasuo or Nobuo along, and so he would head off without a destination.

He often did this on **Saturday** afternoons, after school had adjourned in the morning and he, his mother, and Yasuo had eaten lunch together. He would leave the house with the excuse that he was "going to play with Nobuo."

He loved Saturday afternoons. Everybody did, of course, because work and school had ended and Sunday was a holiday. To Kazuo, time seemed to pass more slowly. The whole town appeared to take a collective deep breath and sprawl out on the floor, forgetting the week's troubles. Walking around Tokyo as it exhaled this way was something Kazuo deeply enjoyed. Sometimes, he crossed the Haneto River, with its stench of factory wastewater that made him want to plug his nose, and headed toward Hara. Other times, he walked past the big houses on the hill in District 4, where he had

Saturday

Japanese public schools held classes on some or all Saturday mornings for many years. Workers often also worked a half-day on Saturdays. Saturday has been a public school holiday since 2002.

Tokyo

The main area of the city of Tokyo (population 13 million) is made up of 23 municipalities, commonly called "wards." Shinagawa Ward, where Kazuo lives, is in the southeastern section of Tokyo and is considered a working-class area.

Tokyo Tower

A tall communications and observation tower in central Tokyo. Inspired by the Eiffel Tower in Paris, it is 1,091 feet (332 meters) high. It was built in 1958 to host antennas for Tokyo's growing broadcast industry in the postwar period. It is now a popular tourist destination.

seen Minoru and his father hauling their scrap cart, and ventured as far as the next ward. Or he went through the West Ito shopping area, where Nobuo's house was, and walked the maze of narrow alleyways behind it, which was where Nishino-kun lived.

He had recently begun to realize that the streets of **Tokyo** were changing. They had been changing, it seemed, ever since the Tokyo Olympics the year before last.

Dirt roads that had filled with puddles when it rained had been paved over, and old wooden houses had been knocked down and replaced with new stucco homes. **Tokyo Tower**, whose red iron tip Kazuo had once been able to see from the District 4 hill, had become invisible, probably because so many new buildings now blocked it from view. Just as Father's older brother Yoshio had said when he visited their family before New Year's, construction had been going on all over Tokyo before the Olympics. Huge stadiums had been built, highways had been routed through the center of the city, and the fastest bullet train in the world had begun regular service between Tokyo and Osaka.

Then again, the construction of new buildings was not

the only reason Tokyo Tower was harder to see. Kazuo had learned on the TV news that exhaust fumes from cars were dirtying the air. He himself had observed that the number of cars on the road was increasing at a very high rate.

He used to be able to cross National Highway One, which intersected the south end of the West Ito shopping area, even with no pedestrian crossing signal. But now there were so many cars that walking across the highway without a signal was impossible.

He did not feel that all this change was bad. Car fumes dirtying the air was certainly a problem, but the tall buildings and automobiles showed that Japan was becoming wealthier. At school, the students still had to drink that awful *miruku*, but that was a different story.

A busy intersection in Shinagawa Ward.

Pachinko

A kind of vertical pinball machine. A steel ball is launched into the top, and as it drops down the face of the board it hits against pins and bumpers. If it falls into a pocket along the way you win additional balls, and the more balls you win the better the reward at the end. *Pachinko* machines are loud with flashing lights and are mostly found at *pachinko* "parlors," noisy arcades that may have hundreds of machines all blinking and beeping at once.

One Saturday, Kazuo finished lunch and told his mother that he was going to the lot to play. Then he began to walk in the direction of the West Ito shopping area, the January wind gusting around him. There was still plenty of time before the late-afternoon rush, when the area would bustle with shoppers. Only a few people passed him on the street now.

He reached the center of the shopping area and saw Takahashi Meats, the shop owned by Nobuo's family. He could smell the delicious aroma of croquettes and see Nobuo's mother frying them at the front of the store. Nobuo was nowhere to be seen. Maybe he was in the back mashing boiled potatoes for the croquettes. Or maybe he was upstairs where the family lived, shirking his chores and getting lost in a comic book.

Whatever the case, Kazuo did not want to be noticed, so he crossed the street and walked quickly past the Takahashis' shop. He glanced back. Still busy frying the croquettes, Nobuo's mother did not seem to have noticed him. He exhaled softly and headed for the train station, feeling a little guilty.

Next to the station was Chujiya, the bar where his father often stopped on his way home. Smoke would be billowing from the *yakitori* chicken barbecue by late afternoon, but right now the doors were closed. Two buildings down, at the *pachinko* hall, he could hear music and the constant clicking of metal balls.

Until last year, the *pachinko* hall had been a cinema called the Ito Theater. It had shown movies for children during the school holidays, and it was here that the children of West Ito had watched, on the edge of their seats, as **Godzilla** took on **Mothra** and **King Ghidorah** and **King Kong** and wreaked havoc in the cities of Japan.

But in the spring of the previous year, the Ito Theater had suddenly closed. That had come as a big shock to Kazuo. Father said it was because everybody had gotten a TV set and stopped going out to the theaters.

Godzilla, Mothra, King Ghidorah

Japanese movie monsters popular in the 1960s. Godzilla would destroy things by stomping on them or smashing them with his tail, or by burning them with his atomic fire breath. Mothra resembled a giant butterfly or moth. She (Mothra is considered a female) is sometimes a friend to and sometimes an enemy of Godzilla. King Ghidorah was a dragonlike creature from outer space with two legs, three heads on long necks, large wings, and two tails.

King Kong

A giant ape from American films that became popular around the world. The movie *King Kong vs. Godzilla* was produced in 1962.

"Used to be we didn't have any TV at all, so movies and plays were the best entertainment there was. Week in and week out, people would look up which movie stars were in which movies and then go out to see them."

Father spoke while staring at the TV's tiny black-and-white screen. A samurai was fending off his attackers.

"Even the tiniest towns had a movie theater or two," he continued. "So you could see a movie close to home, and it didn't cost very much. But now there's a TV set in every house. Nobody bothers going to the theater anymore, unless

Kamishibai

Japanese "paper theater." *Kamishibai* grew popular in the 1930s and involved a performer/narrator visiting a neighborhood and setting up a wooden stage, where he would tell a story using picture cards to illustrate the action. Many times the story would end in a cliffhanger to make sure the audience would come to the next show. The performer sold candy and traveled from town to town or block to block. As Japan modernized and TV took over, *kamishibai* became old-fashioned and died out. (But TV itself was first called *denki kamishibai*, or electric *kamishibai*!)

there's a movie they really want to see. It's no wonder the little local cinemas are hurting for business.

"TV has its good points and its bad points," he added, "but there's nothing you can do about the times changing."

Now, listening to the clicking of metal balls through the glass in the *pachinko* hall's front door, Kazuo found himself remembering how a **kamishibai** man used to perform on Tuesdays in a side street near company housing.

Those *kamishibai* performances, in which the man told stories while showing colorfully illustrated panels in a wooden stage, were one of Kazuo's greatest delights.

The *kamishibai* man always came at three o'clock on Tuesdays, carrying illustrated *kamishibai* cards and cheap sweets in a big wooden box on the back of his black bicycle. When he arrived, he would bang his wooden clappers together to summon the children. Then the children would pay five yen apiece for wafer-thin rice crackers spread with just the tiniest bit of apricot jam, syrup, or savory sauce.

After a group of children had bought their sweets, the man would raise the top portion of his wooden box to create a stage. He would then slide his illustrated cards into and out of the stage as he performed a *kamishibai*. Sometimes, he told adventure stories about the young ninja **Sarutobi Sasuke** or the **Golden Bat**—"a friend of justice who fights evil." Other times, the children heard about a young girl in search of her long-lost mother, or about the funny Happy-Go-Lucky Boy, or they enjoyed quizzes. The *kamishibai* man had different voices for different characters, and the children would be completely drawn into the world of the story that unfolded before them. The performances probably lasted only ten or fifteen minutes, but to Kazuo, they were as thrilling as a one- or two-hour movie.

Around the time he started school, however, the *kamishibai* man had stopped coming. That was just before Kazuo's family got a TV set, on which American shows such as *Father Knows Best*, *Popeye the Sailor*, and *Tom and Jerry*, and Japanese-made programs such as *Moonlight Mask* were being broadcast every day. These programs were not necessarily more interesting than *kamishibai*, but it was easier to stay home and watch the performances on the black-and-white screen.

After he left the *pachinko* parlor, Kazuo walked along a road that followed the train tracks. Right next to him, a train of four cars sped off into the distance with its caution

Sarutobi Sasuke

A legendary ninja in Japanese folklore. Ninja are spies who dress all in black and perform amazing acrobatic feats to scale walls and trees. Known for his agility, Sarutobi Sasuke is said to have been raised by monkeys in the wild (the name "Sarutobi" means "monkey jump").

Golden Bat

A Japanese superhero from the 1930s. Golden Bat is perhaps the first Japanese superhero. He was said to have come from the lost culture of Atlantis to protect the modern world from evil. He had a very muscular body, a red cape, and a skull for a face, and he carried a powerful scepter that could create lightning and earthquakes.

whistle blowing. The fact that Tokyo was quickly changing, and that the movie theater and *kamishibai* man had disappeared, was not something he could blame entirely on the Olympics or TV, he realized. He himself, and Nobuo and Yasuo, and Mother and Father, and the many people living around them, had begun to prefer the new Tokyo over the old. He wondered if this was good or bad.

And if he knew one thing for sure, it was that his city would continue to change.

FEBRUARY

Boys playing rock-paper-scissors on brand-new playground equipment.

A Farewell in the Snow

That February brought fifteen centimeters of snow, which for Tokyo was a very heavy snowfall.

It began snowing on February 3, which was **Setsubun**, the day before the first day of spring. On Setsubun, members of every household shouted, "Out with demons, in with good fortune!" Then they scattered dried soybeans around the house to ward off bad luck.

Kazuo's family was no exception. Every Setsubun, Father would leave work promptly and come straight home, without stopping at the *yakitori* bar by the station. Then Mother, Kazuo, and Yasuo would face Father, who put on a demon mask that Kazuo and Yasuo had made, and they would shout, "Out with demons!" and toss beans at him. Father would cry, "Ouch, ouch!" very dramatically and run from the kitchen to Kazuo and Yasuo's room, then to the living room, and then outside. Once the demon had been chased outside, Father would remove the mask and the entire family would stand in front of the

Setsubun

Bean-throwing ceremony day, February 3. In the old calendar Setsubun was associated with the Lunar New Year, so it was a time for chasing away the evils of the past and welcoming in good fortune. Roasted soybeans are tossed at a family member wearing a demon mask while everyone yells *Oni wa soto! Fuku wa uchi!* ("Out with demons! In with good fortune!"). The "demon" then runs away, and the family munches on more beans to gather in the luck they hope to have in the year ahead.

open front door, chanting, "In with good fortune, in with good fortune," inviting good fortune in by sprinkling more beans.

Running all over the house and sprinkling beans while shouting, "Out with demons, in with good fortune!" was a lot of fun. So Setsubun was one of the annual rituals that Kazuo and Yasuo particularly liked.

But even on Setsubun, there was nothing harder than getting up in the cold of the winter morning.

After Mother yanked off their blankets and shouted, "All right, up and at 'em, you two!" Kazuo and Yasuo had to change clothes in their drafty room, which was only a little bit warmer than the outdoors.

In the living room, Father was already at the *kotatsu*, drinking **tea** while reading the newspaper.

"Today's Setsubun, isn't it? I'll be home by half past six, so be sure to get the demon mask ready by then."

"Maybe this year I'll be a demon, too," Kazuo said, rubbing his hands together underneath the *kotatsu*. He enjoyed pelting his father with beans while shouting, "Out with demons!" But dressing up like a demon and yelling, "Ouch, ouch!" while running all over the place also seemed like fun.

"I'll be the demon, too!" Yasuo said, copying Kazuo as usual.

"No way, you're still a kid," Kazuo said, rapping Yasuo on the head.

"Oww! Stop it, Niichan, you're still a kid, too!"

"Both of you, stop. That's no way to start the day." Mother brought their breakfast on a tray.

Both boys slouched over the *kotatsu*.

Stupid Yasuo. If he'd just quit copying me I wouldn't get in trouble with Okaasan first thing in the morning, Kazuo thought. He wanted to give Yasuo another knock on the head, but he knew Mother would get really upset if he did. He waited until she had put the *miso* soup bowls on the table. Then he stuck his tongue out at Yasuo.

> **Tea**
>
> Japanese are great tea drinkers, although coffee is now very popular, too. Many Japanese families keep large thermoses of hot tea on hand so they can drink it at any time during the day. Tea is very important in Japanese culture, particularly for its role in the tea ceremony, which is a ritualized way of preparing and sharing tea with guests. Types of tea include *matcha*, the tea-ceremony tea, very bitter but used to flavor ice cream and even chocolate bars; *genmaicha*, or brown rice tea; *hojicha*, green tea roasted over charcoal; and *shincha*, or "new tea," made of freshly picked new leaves.

Father left the house right after breakfast at half past seven, and Mother headed to work just before eight o'clock. Before she left, she laid out hand-knitted wool mufflers and mittens for Kazuo and Yasuo.

"We might get snow this afternoon, so be sure you put these on when you go to school so you don't catch colds. And don't forget to take your umbrellas with you, all right?"

"Snow!"

Kazuo and Yasuo were both thrilled at the thought of snow, even though they hated wearing the mufflers and mittens. That was because if they wore them, they would get teased about being mama's boys when they got to school.

They headed to school, leaving behind both the umbrellas and the mufflers and mittens. The sky was covered with thick, gray clouds, and a cold wind stung their cheeks. The adults who were walking in the street were all clearly wearing an extra layer of clothing, looking like a parade of fat, round snowmen. Kazuo and Yasuo wore only their usual winter sweaters plus windbreakers. Their breath was so white that it looked like Godzilla's radioactive breath. They laughed aloud, breathing radioactive breath on each other as they hurried down the road to school.

As they neared the front gate, still horsing around, they spotted Nobuo.

"*Oo-i*, Nobuo!"

Nobuo turned when he heard Kazuo's voice. But instead of flaring his round nostrils in his usual easygoing grin, he waved with almost no expression. He had a dark brown muffler wrapped around his neck.

"*Oi*, what happened to you? You've even got a muffler on," Kazuo said teasingly.

"What was I supposed to do? My mom wouldn't stop harping about it." Nobuo yanked off the muffler and wrapped it around his left hand.

"Our mom told us to wear mufflers and mittens, too, but we didn't!" Yasuo bragged.

"My mom and dad are at home, running the shop all day long," Nobuo reminded them. "So they can check what I'm wearing when I leave."

Kazuo said good-bye to Yasuo and went to his classroom with Nobuo.

"Did you hear that it's supposed to snow this afternoon?" he asked.

Nobuo's eyes went wide with excitement. "Let's meet at the empty lot to sled later. I'll get a tangerine crate from the greengrocer across the street from us." He spotted their other friends. "*Oi*, Minoru, Nishiyan, did you hear? It's supposed to snow this afternoon."

"Yeah, we heard," Minoru said.

"Let's make a snow house," Nishino-kun said.

"That sounds fun." Kazuo remembered Father talking about how people in his village used to have a good time in winter by building snow houses and making fires inside. Then they'd grill rice dumplings and drink sweet *sake*.

He glanced toward the window. The sky was thick with gray clouds, but it had not yet started snowing. Soon, the bell rang, and Mr. Honda came into the classroom. He had lit the stove, but the room wasn't very warm yet. Still, no one complained about the cold. That was because they all knew that snow was coming.

For a long time, nothing happened. But just after eleven thirty, when the smell of lunch began to drift into the classroom, the first flake came fluttering down, drifting to the left and right. When it touched the dried dirt of the schoolyard, it quickly faded away.

"Hey, it's snowing!" someone yelled.

The eyes of every student shifted to the world outside the window, and every mouth formed the same word: "Snow!"

Mr. Honda smiled.

"Okay, everybody, for three minutes, go to the windows and have a look at the snow. But when three minutes are up, we're starting class again."

At his words, the forty students all scrambled to the windows.

Kazuo saw that the snow was beginning to fall a bit harder. But not hard enough, he thought. Around him, a few of the others had noticed the same thing. "I hope this snow sticks," a girl murmured. Everybody in the class nodded in agreement.

At two in the afternoon, school ended and the students stepped into the schoolyard to find that the snow was beginning to accumulate. But when Kazuo tried to scoop up some, it melted instantly.

After he made sure that Yasuo was headed home, he went to the empty lot as usual with Nobuo, Nishino-kun, and Minoru. None of them had an umbrella. There was still not enough snow to make snowmen or have a snowball fight, let alone sled on tangerine crates.

"If it keeps falling like this, it should be pretty deep in the morning," Nishino-kun said.

"Yeah, you're right." Minoru nodded. "Let's all come back at six thirty in the morning. We can play until school starts."

"That's a good idea." Nobuo was the first to agree. "I'll bring the tangerine crate then for sledding."

Kazuo decided he would bring Yasuo along as a treat. Promising to meet the next morning, he and his three friends parted ways.

At home, Yasuo had taken out a thick piece of drawing paper and was making a red demon mask for their Setsubun celebration.

"How about we make two demon masks this year?" Kazuo said, putting down his bag and tucking into the *kotatsu*.

"Hmm, how about a blue demon?"

"That sounds good. Red and blue are a good combination."

Using the rest of the drawing paper, Kazuo made a blue demon mask.

"Are you going to be a demon this year, Oniichan?" Yasuo asked.

"Do you want to be one, too?"

Yasuo pursed his lips and acted like he was thinking for a moment. Then he gave a small nod.

"You do nothing but copy me, you know that?" Kazuo laughed, poking Yasuo lightly in the head.

Once they had finished the demon masks, the two boys hunkered down at the *kotatsu* and read comics, checking the condition of the snow every thirty minutes. By the time their mother got home and the Imamura Tofu man had come to sell tofu, there was finally enough to cover Kazuo's canvas shoes. Kazuo and Yasuo put on rubber boots and hurried outside, building a small snowman in front of the house.

Father came home earlier than expected.

"I bet this snow will get pretty deep," he said from the entryway as he brushed snow off his shoulders.

Yasuo hurried to meet him. "How do you know?"

"Because the air feels chilly and moist," Father said,

Miso — A flavoring paste, usually made with soybeans and a fermenting agent. *Miso* soup usually contains *miso*, hot water, green onions, and bits of tofu. It often accompanies a traditional Japanese meal.

rubbing his hands together. He sat down at the *kotatsu*. "You know that rain turns to snow when the air is cold, right? And when the air is moist, we get moist, sticky snowflakes and very heavy snow. But enough about that. Today is Setsubun. Did you make the demon mask like I told you?"

"Look, Oniichan and I made two!" Yasuo showed Father the red and blue demon masks they had made on drawing paper.

"Wow, double demons this year!" Father laughed.

"Dinner's ready, so help me bring it out," Mother called to Kazuo and Yasuo from the kitchen.

Dinner that night was croquettes, boiled tofu, and *miso* soup with onion.

"Hey, these aren't croquettes from Nobuo-chan's place, are they?" Yasuo said.

Kazuo had chewed off a bite of his and agreed that it didn't taste at all like the ones from Nobuo's shop. The Takahashis' croquettes had a lot of ground meat in them, and the potatoes and onions weren't mashed up like these were.

"Nobuo-chan's shop wasn't open today. Anyway, I bought these at the butcher shop by the station," Mother said. "Eat up, boys. And no complaints."

Kazuo silently ate the croquette from the butcher by the station and drank the *miso* soup with onion that he did not particularly like, and brought a little bit of the boiled tofu to his mouth.

And then, just as he got ready to down the rest of the tofu, they heard a knock on the door.

"Good evening! Is Kazuo-kun here?"

"Nobuo?" Kazuo put his chopsticks down and went to the entryway.

Nobuo stood there, covered in snowflakes and heaving his shoulders as he breathed hard.

"What happened?" Kazuo said, startled.

"Nothing . . . I just . . . uh . . . something came up . . . and . . ." Nobuo spoke in short bursts while trying to catch his breath.

"*Oi*, are you all right? Slow down a little." Kazuo beckoned Nobuo into the entryway.

"Yeah, I'm fine." Nobuo took two deep breaths. "Listen, you know how we all promised to meet at the lot tomorrow morning? It looks like I won't be able to make it, and I felt bad since we promised, so I came to tell you that I'm sorry." Perhaps because of the cold, Nobuo's lips looked paler than usual. "And I was wondering if you could tell Nishiyan and Minoru for me."

"What's wrong, Nobuo-chan?" Mother came to the entryway. "It's cold out. Why don't you come inside instead of standing here?"

"It's all right, thanks. I have to get home really soon." Nobuo bowed his head to Kazuo's mother, and she went back to the dinner table.

"Sorry about tomorrow," Nobuo said again to Kazuo. "But I asked the greengrocer about the tangerine box. You should use it and go sledding."

"We can always do that some other time. We'll get more snow and then everybody can go sledding together."

"Yeah, that's true. Right." Nobuo flared his nostrils and flashed his usual grin. "Also, I was wondering if you could tell Mr. Honda something for me tomorrow. I have to go to my dad's home in the countryside, so I won't be able to come to school for a while."

Kazuo was surprised. "What happened, is there a funeral?"

"Uh, well . . ." Nobuo flushed. "Something like that."

"So that's why your shop was closed today," Kazuo said, nodding. "My mom had to buy some croquettes from the butcher shop by the station. They're no good at all. The croquettes from your place are definitely the best."

"Really? The best, huh?" Nobuo smiled bashfully. "Well, then, I've got to go."

"Bye," Kazuo said.

Nobuo nodded and ran off into the snow. A second later, Kazuo saw him stop.

"I'm going to tell my dad what you said," he called back to Kazuo. "That you think our croquettes are the best!" Nobuo stood under an old street lamp. The soft lamplight lit up the snow as it fell, making it glint like needles. Kazuo waved a hand at his friend. Nobuo waved back and then disappeared into the falling snow.

When Kazuo returned to the table, Mother, Father, and Yasuo had finished their dinner.

"What happened to Nobuo-chan?" Mother asked.

"He said he has to go to a relative's funeral and won't be

able to come to school for a while. He wants me to tell Mr. Honda." In a stroke of good fortune, all of the tofu had been eaten, so Kazuo could get away with eating just his croquette for dinner.

When he was finished, Father stood up. "Well, why don't we scatter the beans for Setsubun, then?" Kazuo and Yasuo jumped right up.

"You two can be the demons first," Father said, handing the masks to the boys.

Kazuo and Yasuo met each other's eyes and grinned. At last, they could have the more grown-up job! They both put the masks on triumphantly. Yasuo instantly started stalking around the house with his fingers bent, like Godzilla, yelling, "*Rarrrr, rarrr.*"

"*Oi*, Yasuo," said Father. "Today you're not supposed to be Godzilla, you're supposed to be a Setsubun demon!" Mother picked up a wooden measuring cup with beans in it. "All right, then, you two know what's coming."

"Here we go!" Beans in hand, Father took aim at Kazuo and Yasuo, and lightly tossed the beans, shouting, "Out with demons!" The beans hit Kazuo's shoulder, and then scattered on the kitchen floor.

"Out with demons!" called Mother. Then she scattered some beans in the direction of the boys.

Kazuo and Yasuo dramatically yelled, "Ouch, ouch!" and ran from the kitchen to their own room, and then to the living room. They ran to all of the rooms in the house, getting pelted by the beans. Finally, they left the house through the entryway and went outside.

The snow was even deeper now, completely covering Kazuo's ankles.

"Your father and I are next." Mother took the red demon mask from Yasuo. After Kazuo handed his blue mask to Father, everyone went back in the house. This time, Kazuo and Yasuo yelled, "Out with demons!" while tossing beans at Father and Mother. Their parents cried, "Ouch, ouch!" and ran through the house while Kazuo and Yasuo howled with laughter and chased after them with the beans.

Then, after Father and Mother left through the entryway just as Kazuo and Yasuo had done, the boys followed them outside. Father and Mother removed the masks, and the entire family lined up in front of the house. Each of them took a handful of beans from the cup that Father was holding. Facing the entryway, they shouted, "In with good fortune!" and scattered the beans.

All around them, Kazuo could hear other voices yelling, "Out with demons! In with good fortune!" He wondered if Nobuo's family had had time to scatter beans before leaving for the countryside.

Father looked up at the snow falling from the night sky. "Scattering the beans in the snow is nice, isn't it?"

"Yes," Kazuo agreed, sticking out his tongue to catch some of the flakes.

The next morning, Kazuo woke before his alarm clock rang. Sticking his head from inside his bedding, he felt the chilly air in the house. The room seemed to glow a bright white. "Yasuo, wake up!" He shook Yasuo, who was still fast asleep, buried in his bedding. "It's six o'clock. We're going to the lot."

"I wonder if the snow got deep," Yasuo said drowsily, poking his head out.

"I bet it did." Being careful not to wake Father and Mother, who were sleeping in the living room, Kazuo quietly changed his clothes. It was so cold that he and Yasuo ordinarily wouldn't get out of their bedding for anything, but today it was no trouble at all. Putting on a thick shirt and round-necked sweater, with his windbreaker over the top, Kazuo opened the papered sliding door of the bedroom and tiptoed around the edge of the living room. Yasuo was right behind him.

"Kazuo, is that you?" called Mother.

"Yes."

"Where are you going so early?" She stuck her face out from under her blanket.

"To the lot."

"You can't move a muscle in the morning when I take your blanket off, but today you're already up and dressed? It figures," she said in a sleepy-sounding voice. "Today you *will* wear the mufflers and mittens that are on the *kotatsu*. And I put your rubber boots out, so put those on. And you absolutely must be back by seven fifteen to have some breakfast before school. Do you understand?"

She pointed at the *kotatsu* that had been moved to a corner of the room. On it were the mufflers and mittens that Kazuo and Yasuo had not taken to school the day before.

The two boys nodded obediently and then wrapped the mufflers around their necks and slipped the mittens on. Looking through the glass front door, Kazuo realized that the snow had grown much deeper. When he opened the door, the bright light practically blinded him.

"Oniichan, this is amazing, isn't it?" Yasuo said.

Everything was covered with snow as far as they could see. The snow had stopped falling, but the street in front of the house was covered in a thick blanket of white. Kazuo stepped into the fresh snow. His boot sank until the snow was at his knee.

Yasuo followed Kazuo and took a step. "Wow, I can't believe it!"

The boys walked along slowly, stepping in the spots where the snow was deepest.

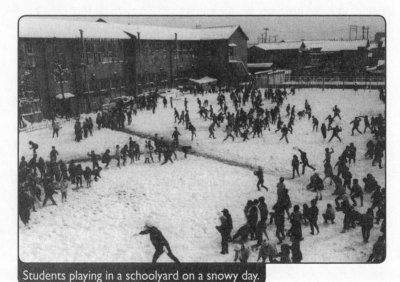
Students playing in a schoolyard on a snowy day.

When they turned onto the main road, they saw a number of tire tracks. The two boys began to hurry to the empty lot.

No one else was there yet. Kazuo grabbed Yasuo's arm and ran around in the pure white snow, yelling at the top of his lungs. Then, when he was tired of running, he made a snowball and threw it far away. He marveled at how his breath was even whiter than yesterday. Soon, Nishino-kun and Minoru showed up. Just like Kazuo and Yasuo, they wore mufflers around their necks and had mittens on.

Nishino-kun looked at Kazuo. "Where's Takahashi-kun?"

"Last night he came to my place and said they had to go to his relatives' house. He can't come today, so he told me to apologize to you two," Kazuo said.

"Really? That's too bad." Minoru pursed his lips.

After that, the four boys made snowmen, had a snowball fight, and used some old boards left in the corner of the lot as sleds. At last, they all knew it was time to go home to get ready for school.

Mother scolded Kazuo and Yasuo when she saw that they were covered with snow. They quickly changed into different clothes. The TV news was reporting that traffic in downtown Tokyo was at a standstill.

"Tokyo really falls apart when it snows," Father murmured. "I wonder if the trains are stopped, too."

After he and Mother had both left for work, Kazuo and Yasuo headed to school. A few soft beams of sunlight were beginning to appear through breaks in the clouds.

Mr. Honda arrived thirty minutes later than usual.

Kazuo and his classmates played in the schoolyard during that time, making snowmen and having snowball fights. The snow began to grow slightly wet and slushy in their hands.

Before class started, Kazuo told Mr. Honda Nobuo's news. Mr. Honda smiled cheerfully as always, then said, "Thank you, I understand," and proceeded to start the lesson.

But during lunch period that day, when Kazuo was plugging his nose and drinking his disgusting *miruku*, a girl in his class came to tell him that Mr. Honda wanted to see him in the teachers' room.

"It's about Takahashi-kun," said Mr. Honda. "When he mentioned his relatives, did he say which ones they were?"

"I think he said they were going to visit his father's relatives in the country," Kazuo answered.

"I see.... Thank you very much," Mr. Honda said politely.

Outside, at recess, any thoughts of snow had vanished from Kazuo's head. Instead, Mr. Honda's question about Nobuo weighed heavily on his mind.

After school ended, Kazuo took Nishino-kun and Minoru with him to Takahashi Meats. The melted snow had wet the asphalt, making it look very black.

When they reached Nobuo's house, the door to the butcher shop was shut. A sheet of paper was taped to the door.

"We have enjoyed your patronage for many years, but today we close our doors. We express our gratitude to the shoppers of West Ito and to all of our neighbors in this commercial district. We hope for the continued prosperity and development of West Ito. Owners, Takahashi Meats, February 3."

"What's going on?" Minoru asked anxiously.

"Yesterday, when he talked to you, did Takahashi-kun say anything about this?" Nishino-kun asked Kazuo.

"No, nothing," Kazuo said. "Just that something had come up and the family was going to his relatives' house." Then he happened to remember Nobuo saying he would ask the greengrocer for a tangerine box.

They headed across the street.

"Excuse me, **my name is Nakamoto**. I'm a classmate of Nobuo, the son of the butcher across the road," Kazuo told the man who was lining up vegetables with a cigarette in his mouth.

"Ah, a friend of Nobuo's, are you?" The vegetable man turned and said, "If you've come about the tangerine crates, they're right over there. You can take as many as you want."

Nobuo had made a point of asking the greengrocer for the crates. Kazuo suddenly felt like breaking down in tears. "Excuse me, do you know what happened at Takahashi-kun's place? Did they close up the store?"

"Oh, yes. Didn't you hear?" the man said. "Seems somebody found out they were mixing cheap rabbit meat with the

---

"My name is Nakamoto"

Generally Japanese people introduce themselves by giving their family name only, without any kind of respectful suffix. So Kazuo simply introduces himself as "Nakamoto." English speakers usually introduce themselves by their first or full names. (In Japan, the family name comes first—Kazuo's name in Japan is Nakamoto Kazuo—but this book gives the family name last to avoid confusion.)

pork they sold. The fellow who ran it wasn't a bad sort, but he must have had a weak moment."

"Do you know when they'll be coming back?" Minoru asked.

"They probably won't come back here, son. They cheated their customers." The man blew smoke toward the sky.

The boys nodded but didn't say a word. They walked back to the entrance of the shopping area. From there, they had to walk in different directions to go home.

"Nobuo will be back, won't he?" Minoru said in a small voice.

I bet he never will, Kazuo thought. But somehow he felt that if he said that aloud, Nobuo really would never return.

"Let's ask Mr. Honda tomorrow about what to do," Nishino-kun said.

The others nodded. Then, briefly raising their hands in a wave, they walked off in different directions.

Kazuo felt like crying, but no tears fell. He had lost his good friend, the one who could help him figure out how to run like Bob Hayes.

He stared at the snow melting all around him. Then he remembered how happy Nobuo had sounded when Kazuo told him that his family's croquettes were the best.

Maybe he'd been able to tell himself that his father was not a bad man after all.

MARCH / APRIL

First day of school for a first-grade class in April.

Kazuo's Journey

In mid-March, Minoru moved away from West Ito like No-buo before him, and Kazuo lost another friend.

Mr. Honda announced to the fourth-grade class that, due to a repatriation program for North Koreans in Japan, Minoru and his family had decided to return to their home country of North Korea, across the sea to the west. Then Mr. Honda asked Minoru to say a few words of farewell. Minoru looked a little self-conscious, standing up in front of the entire class.

"Everyone in grade four section three, thank you for everything. Even though I am returning to my fatherland, I will never forget West Ito Elementary School. I will be sure to write to everyone when I arrive, so please write to me as well."

The class applauded for Minoru and sang the West Ito Elementary School song to cheer his departure.

Not long after that, a single letter arrived from Minoru and was posted on the back wall of the classroom. The name

Korean phonetic letters

The official script of North and South Korea, *hangul*, was created in the mid-15th century. Each *hangul* character forms a sound.

of the sender was written with different characters than Kazuo knew from before, but the handwriting was definitely Minoru's. The letter said, "Dear Everyone at West Ito Elementary School, how have you been? I am studying very hard every day to contribute to my fatherland."

Kazuo and Nishino-kun immediately sent a reply to Minoru's address, which was written in difficult ideographs and **Korean phonetic letters** that looked like strange symbols. They told Minoru all the news at their school and asked him whether there was *sumo* wrestling in North Korea. But another reply from Minoru never came.

In **April**, a new term began, and Kazuo became a fifth grader. He was still in section three of his grade, but his teacher was a woman, Mrs. Yamazaki. Nishino-kun had been placed in section one.

Kazuo sat on a patch of soft grass in the empty lot, which had finally begun to turn green. He gazed far off over the rooftops of nearby houses to a corner of the schoolyard, where a cherry tree was in bloom. Kazuo looked up at the sky. Its clear blue stretched on forever, as far as he could see.

From the autumn of 1965 through the winter months, many of the people closest to him had vanished. Mr. Yoshino's tofu shop had been turned into a store that sold electric appliances. A new butcher shop had opened up where Nobuo's family had lived (the croquettes weren't nearly as good as Nobuo's family's). And the house that Minoru had left was still a vacant black skeleton, without any sign of life.

> **April**
>
> The month when school begins in Japan. Japanese students go to school almost all year round, with a shorter summer vacation and time off at New Year's. Students also wear uniforms, wool in the winter and cotton in the hotter months.

Kazuo spied some white clouds like wisps of cotton candy drifting in from the south. They were moving at a constant, steady pace.

To him, the clouds looked a bit like a camel making a journey through the desert. Astride the camel, between its two humps, sat a young man with a white cloth wrapped around his head in Middle Eastern fashion. No doubt, he had journeyed alone through the desert for many days, making his way to a land far off in the east.

The desert traveler probably feared that he would end up a pile of dried skin and bones, such as he had seen here and there along his path. Remembering the warm affection of the people he had left behind, he had to fight the urge to hurry back to the safety of his home. But like a movie hero, he continued his perilous journey. Around him stretched endless dry, cracked earth and craggy mountains. Ahead, he hoped to glimpse a magnificent palace decorated in silver and gold.

Kazuo gazed at the sky and pictured himself as a questing traveler.

Though he imagined that somewhere beyond the sky he could see the landscape of a foreign country, he knew that it was probably very different from the far-off countries shown on TV. In those images, each home had vivid green grass in the yard, a living room with a fireplace and roomy sofa, a private room and a bed for each person, and a huge refrigerator stuffed with more food than you could ever eat. There were jugs of milk so big that you would have to wrap both arms around them to pick them up, skyscrapers so tall that they stuck through the sky, gigantic cars, freeways that went on forever, and the *hanbaagaa* that Wimpy ate. . . .

But Kazuo was beginning to realize that foreign countries had disturbing as well as beautiful scenery. He thought of Vietnam, where there were air raids almost every day and people were running for their lives; of Africa, where children his own age were starving and dying one after another, their stomachs grossly swollen; and of North Korea, where Minoru had gone with his family, and had mysteriously fallen out of touch. Those were foreign countries, too.

And in those places, it was not true that everything was always pleasant and wonderful. Suffering and sorrow had existed, and probably continued to exist, as daily realities, just like they did in Japan—or even far more than they did here.

Kazuo stood and brushed the seat of his pants, sweeping away moist earth that smelled of new grass. The cloud camel and traveler had passed over his head and at some point had lost their shape. He stared in their direction.

"Someday, I will leave this city and this country. I'll meet many other people who left the places where they were born, like me."

Thinking about it made Kazuo's heart leap a little in his chest.

Maybe by that time, his father would no longer get drunk and tell him to enter a national university, earn a degree at graduate school, and work at a top company. And maybe his mother would no longer say "during the war," and would have mended her ties with Kazuo's grandfather. And just maybe, Yasuo would finally be raising the dog he had waited and waited for. And as for Kazuo himself . . .

For now, he still lived in a world called Tokyo.

He looked out at his city. The small houses huddled closely together, like a group of animals still sleeping on a meadow in early spring. Soon, they would feel the warmth of the sun, and they would start their journey toward a new green field.

Kazuo felt he could run as fast as a four-legged animal, perhaps a gazelle. He took a breath of fresh spring air and sprinted off toward the horizon.

Students racing at a middle-school sports day.

An Author's Note to His Readers

I wrote this book while remembering my own childhood in Tokyo in the 1960s. I knew boys like Kazuo and his friends— the J-Boys—and the area where I lived (and still live) was very much like West Ito in Shinagawa Ward. I wanted to show how Japanese kids were influenced by American culture back then. Even the Beatles were influenced by American rock and roll—Little Richard, Chuck Berry, and of course Elvis.

Everything that happens in this book sort of happened to me—or to my friends, you might say—but not in exactly the way it happens here. Throughout this book, I've added some notes and photographs to help you understand what life was like for me and other kids back then.

I remember the tofu shop, the empty lots and the stray dogs, the American cartoons, the TV shows on black and white screens, and all the noise and construction. There are still tofu shops in Tokyo. But the physical look of Tokyo, except for some side streets and quiet neighborhoods, is nothing like what it was when I was growing up. Nowadays, there aren't so many empty lots. There are no stray dogs, and kids rarely play on side streets (they're more likely inside on their computers, playing video games, or spending time at after-school cram centers). Yes, things change, and in my imagination they have changed a great deal for Kazuo and his friends, too, although I must emphasize that these J-Boys in particular are largely a work of my imagination.

In case you're wondering, Minoru never did write another letter back from North Korea, and no one knows what happened to him or where he is today. I read some newspaper reports of Japanese Koreans who moved to North Korea, as Minoru's family did. Most of them had hard lives there because Japanese-Koreans are considered the lowest members of their society. Still, I hope that Minoru and his family settled comfortably and are doing okay. As for Keiko Sasaki, I'll bet she ended up moving to Switzerland with her Swiss husband. She's probably living a peaceful life with her family in the mountains.

Yasuo had to wait until he grew up and got his own house before he got a dog. And even then it was a small dog, since houses in Japan are still small compared to houses in America. He works for a record company and listens to rock and roll music all day long. Nobuo stayed in the countryside after he and his parents had to leave Tokyo in embarrassment, after a rabbit meat scandal that affected a number of butchers. Once, after Kazuo started working as a businessman at a company, he ran into Nobuo in Osaka. Kazuo took his clients to a sushi bar, and when he saw the short-haired sushi chef, he recognized Nobuo right away. They were both so happy to see each other again. After that, Nobuo married and opened his own sushi bar in Kyushu, southern Japan, where his wife is from. He sends a New Year's card to Kazuo asking about his family every year.

Yes, that's right. Kazuo got married and had kids. He lives in Tokyo now, not too far from where he grew up. He and his wife have a boy and a girl, who love spending time with their Uncle Yasuo. Otohsan and Okaasan passed away a while back, but not before they got to see their grandchildren.

And before Kazuo settled down to work in Japan, he really did get to travel around the world, just as he dreamed of doing when he watched the clouds that day in April, and when he told his friends he wanted to be a ship's captain. He even learned to speak English, and spent some time living in America and England. You remember how he was good at math? Although his father hoped that he would get a Ph.D. in science, Kazuo studied sociology and economics. Of course, his father was disappointed at first, but later managed to satisfy himself that at least Kazuo had gotten into a good college and hadn't flunked out.

Now, as for Nishino-kun, he never did go to college, although he loved to read and write poetry, and from time to time he would send Kazuo a poem he had written. I'm afraid something very sad happened to Nishino-kun, but Kazuo will always remember him as a good friend who gave him wonderful memories. In one of his letters, Nishino-kun wrote to Kazuo, "Live your life fully enough for the both of us."

Kazuo now has gray hair. He has saved that letter from Nishino-kun, and thinks of the J-Boys often. And, speaking of J-Boys, there was a Japanese rock album in the 1980s with the title *J.BOY*. Maybe Yasuo even had something to do with it, but I'll never know for sure.

Shogo Oketani
Tokyo, 2011

Note: The title *J-Boys* is inspired by Shogo Hamada's *J.BOY*, a Japanese rock album released in 1986.

GLOSSARY